A FEW PERSONAL MESSAGES

A FEW PERSONAL MESSAGES

PIERRE CLÉMENTI

TRANSLATED BY CLAIRE FOSTER

WITH AN INTRODUCTION AND AFTERWORD BY BALTHAZAR CLÉMENTI

Copyright © 1973 by S.E.F. Ph. Daudy
Copyright © Editions Gallimard, 2005
Translation copyright © 2022 by Claire Foster
All rights reserved

First edition, 2022

Library of Congress Cataloging-in-Publication Data
ISBN: 978-1-7348382-1-3

Designed by Eric Wrenn Office
Typeset in Sabon by Jan Tschichold

Printed in the United States of America

http://www.smallpressnyc.com

1 3 5 7 9 10 8 6 4 2

For Louis Aragon

Note from the translator:
On page 33, Pierre Clémenti refers to the director of the movie *Necropolis*. In both the original 1973 edition (S.E.F. Ph. Daudy) and the 2005 Folio edition (Gallimard) of *A Few Personal Messages*, the name "Luca Branconi" appears, although the director of this film is Franco Brocani.

CONTENTS

INTRODUCTION BY BALTHAZAR CLÉMENTI	19
NOAH'S ARK	25
SHOOTING STARS	33
THE QUEEN OF THE HEAVENS	41
A LIFELINE TO THE UNKNOWN	57
THE FATHER'S JUDGMENT	63
GREEN FACES	69
SLEEPING BEAUTY	77
THE STONE OF LIFE	83
FAREWELL TO THE IDOL	91
THE ROAD	99
THE ILLUMINATED COURT	105
THE EVENING MAIL	113
A SINGLE SPARK CAN SET ALL PRISONS AFLAME	121
REFUSING OBEDIENCE	129
SEATED IN THE DARK	135
ONE-WAY TICKET	141
DEAR MINISTER OF JUSTICE…	147
AFTERWORD BY BALTHAZAR CLÉMENTI	153

On the morning of July 24, 1971, the doorbell rang at the apartment of Pierre Clémenti's friend, with whom the actor had been staying in Rome. His five-year-old son Balthazar opened the door. Plainclothes police officers had come to search the apartment, knowing full well what they were looking for: a few grams of cocaine and some hashish. (His son later insisted that he had witnessed the police plant the cocaine under the bed and assure him, "It's nothing. Go back to sleep.")

Everything points to the fact that the authorities set out to make a resounding example of Pierre Clémenti, movie star and countercultural icon. His arrest caused quite a stir. Clémenti was held in the Regina Coeli prison under mere suspicion, and he denied ever having known about the drugs. He would have to wait eight months before being sentenced to two years in prison. Clémenti was eventually released, following an appeal, after eighteen months. He was forever haunted by this time in prison.

This book testifies against the Italian penal code that dates back to fascism, against the prison system and societal repression—all in hopes of shining some light and humanity in even the darkest of cells.

—Balthazar Clémenti

A Few Personal Messages

Noah's Ark

"Sir…"

In France, you stand to attention when you talk to the warden. And at your sides, on your heels and heavy-handed, are your two guardian angels, the two guards flanking you as if for an inspection.

"Sir, I would like to have my flute…"

In Italian prisons, all you have to do is be polite to the warden. To speak to him kindly, naturally, as if to an old friend whom you often turn to in need. In France, you must salute, as in the army.

"Sir, I would like to be able to talk to my mother for a little while longer. She travelled more than a thousand miles to see me…"

As soon as you have something to ask for, it's up to the warden. So you pay him a visit. It's an opportunity to change scenery, stretch your legs, and get to know the corridors.

You're also hoping for a little conversation, even if he doesn't talk much. Whether he's from Rebibbia or Regina Coeli, he waits for you to finish what you're saying. He smiles as he listens to you, his face brightens, and this encourages you to go on. He observes you. Then, he'll say yes or no. He'll either grant you a little happiness, or send you back down to your brothers, where you'll be just as powerless as they are. And then you make your way back through the corridors and down the stairs; you pass the iron bars and hear the jingling of keys; you walk as slowly as possible, taking deep breaths, and soon you end up back in your place. Ten feet by ten feet.

"Sir, please let me play the flute. A young French girl sent it to me. You don't dislike music, do you?"

You look him straight in the eyes, with neither hostility nor fear. You hold his gaze so he can't look away. Still, music isn't forbidden, is it? You smile at him. But in France, it's really like the military. If you don't salute, if you don't correct your posture, you're likely to get two weeks in solitary. Or four weeks, depending on his mood and your look. Two weeks (but it feels like years!) alone in your cell, with nothing but yourself, looking for a light that can only come from within. Such are the rules of the game: the salute or the secret.

Here, you're listened to. You are polite, everyone is polite. Yes or no, simple as that.

"The use of musical instruments is permitted only for minors. You aren't a minor, are you, Monsieur Clémenti?

"You look like my father, Sir..."

We are all children here.

* * *

In my Roman prisons, I got to know three wardens.

The first was something of an apostle. A public servant who believed he had a mission. Like a Father Superior of the cloistered, he wanted to change what prisons were. "I want to transform this prison from a place of repression to a place of creation," he would say. Everyone thought this was funny—especially people on the outside, such as city officials or prison administrators—but he wasn't the only one at Rebibbia to believe it. He wanted to set up lawns in the courtyards so inmates would someday be able to invite their wives and children to stretch out next to them on the grass for an afternoon, get some sun, relax before returning to work—back to their debt, as they say. To pay their debt. What kinds of debts, I don't know. But some had debts.

The girl had sent me the flute so I'd have it for Christmas, but I ended up leaving Rebibbia before Christmas. Rebibbia was Rome's model prison; it was liberal and modern, similar to Fleury-Mérogis. Things were better at Rebibbia than at Regina Coeli. But that didn't stop revolts from happening.

"Sir, I won't have time to play this flute. Let me give it to you."

He looked at me and smiled. As he got up, I told him, "For your big family, your thousands of children, you have a choice to make: destroy them, or help them live—following, or not, the Christian values of charity and fraternity. Even the meekest among them are your brothers. And they are beyond repair, because you can never truly leave behind the prison in which you've suffered for too long. You know that the men in your care could be transformed. The State didn't entrust you with these children for you to annihilate them. Perhaps instead you could grant them happiness and uplift their spirits, so they can learn something that will actually help them once they are released—something to prevent them from being systematically doomed to come back here, back to you, back to this hell where they don't belong."

The warden looked at me with surprise.

"I am a teacher. I have learned that the guilty must be convicted, and that the convicted must be kept in tight command."

He didn't say this in a mean way. He reminded me of Vittorio De Sica in his best roles.

I continued, "It's up to you to transform this repressive approach into an educational one. It's your responsibility to create it. But you won't create it alone—you'll create it with all the men down below, sweating in the holds of your ship. If you hurt them today, they'll hurt you tomorrow. And they'll do it because they know that you have the power to do the right thing, and that you're choosing not to. You have a choice."

Now he was silent before the truth: he really had a choice.

After this conversation, the administration tried to get me transferred to a different prison. I had wanted to say things simply, the way a son would speak to his father. Was it because this truth was pronounced in love, not hate, that it seemed so subversive?

My lawyers managed to let me stay in this so-called model prison. I wish someone would actually make a model prison. For now, Rebibbia remains a hellhole in the hands of military men with absolute power.

"Sir, take this flute, and if one day there is another young man in my place, you can show him the pleasure that comes from playing it."

He walked me to the door. He said it was complicated, that he had a lot of problems with his prisoners because they were unruly and fussy, like children. At the door of his office, it occurred to me that walking us prisoners back was part of the role he'd given himself.

What did he end up doing with this flute? Did he give it away, or is it just lying in some drawer, awaiting another lost soul, another traveler, or another warden?

My first warden was too good for Rebibbia. His initiatives put the prison system itself into question. More joy for prisoners—what a crazy idea! The prison inspectorate had him swiftly transferred. Before he left, he gathered us all together and said, simply, "Farewell!" He was replaced by an oppressive warden. But that one didn't last long, either—three revolts in a row and he was gone.

* * *

A revolt in a prison is no ordinary thing—war, dread, the guards' clenched teeth, screams, crashes on the floor, slammed doors, shrill whistles all around you. Routine is broken. Everything is disrupted; orders cease to be heard. The Italian riot police wait outside, armed with rifles and batons, awaiting orders to intervene.

During a revolt, the guards' habits (card games, rounds) are interrupted, and they are scared. Everyone is scared. And the next day, they'll beat you for anything, just to release the excess tension they'd built up in a matter of hours. In the middle of the night, you hear screams surge from the walls of this underworld. The guards lay waste.

After the third revolt, the administration finally understood: the warden was the problem. He was a poor shepherd to his flock. He was fired. This is very different from French prisons where, after a mutiny, the captain stays. He's the one who steers the ship.

A prison is like Noah's Ark, with representatives of all of humanity's races and classes sailing together on a long journey. We are trapped—the flood. We await the return of the doves, bearers of peace and pardon. But in prison, bad news flies in quicker than the good. Even in the most secluded cells of Rebibbia, we knew about the revolts in French prisons and we were happy.

In Italy, our reasons for revolt were in opposition to the penal code, judicial system, and prisons' rules of procedure that dated back to Mussolini. Thirty years was not enough time for them to be truly changed. Hundreds of committees have convened, hundreds of honorable members of Parliament have addressed dozens of governments, all in vain. The fascist code is still standing. And prisoners are up in arms.

We climbed onto the rooftops, as they did in Toul. There were a lot of us—the older prisoners, who were used to setbacks, as well as the entire juvenile wing. It was a beautiful night, a celebration. The Trastevere families came to cheer us on, waving to the occasional friend or parent. We didn't see the guards. They were holed up in the canteens, barricaded as if we were after them, but we just wanted to show the world the deplorable existence we had there. We wanted to break open, just for one night, the prison's walls.

Of course, just as in Toul, the *celeri* were sent to shut us down. We'd known how, in France, the CRS were in charge of solving this kind of problem, and how in just one or two hours, with their batons or tear gas, everything would return to order. So we invited journalists to the show and the *celeri* knew that if they started beating us, there was going to be blood, which wouldn't be very good for the government. Such was the rule of Italy's political game: everything must proceed smoothly. So, we negotiated. Someone from the Minister of Justice made us big promises. And, naturally, we got cheated.

Many of the same police officers and judges who served under Mussolini are still working. And the majority of those in power today once suckled black milk from the fascist teat. When one hears the tunes of Order and Nation every day for twenty years, it takes root somewhere in the back of the brain and never leaves. Of course, with time, these people have separated themselves from fascism. They have renamed themselves Christian-Democrats. They no longer hesitate to publicly denounce the "bad sides" of Mussolini. But that means that there were "good sides" and they haven't forgotten them.

"What do your prisoners want?"

"They are demanding the new code."

This question travels from the rooftops to the court, from the warden to the commissioner. To revolt for one law! If only it was for money, then we could talk.

"Oh, maybe in a year. We can't do it any sooner."

"Then give them something now."

The following night, the guards cornered about eighty guys who were on the rooftops. It was your regular massacre, just another day in prison. One by one, prisoners had sheets thrown over their heads, and the guards beat them up. Eight against one. But the next day, one of the prisoners was put on trial. He didn't need to speak. He opened his shirt and showed his chest to all who had come to the hearing—judges, journalists, family, friends. And at dusk, the mothers and spouses of the prisoners, hundreds of families in total, assembled outside the prison.

We started over.

"Sir, we would like—"

"What do you want now?"

"We would like to see our wives more often. We would like to be able to hug our children, to have the right to touch them."

But they couldn't be bothered. This penal code was here to stay. Every day, dozens of guys were locked up on mere suspicion; hundreds of prisoners like me had to wait eight months, one year, or more, before even entering the courtroom and being fairly tried. During visiting hours, our lawyers told us, "Be patient, minds are changing."

As we returned to our cells, we looked around at one another. "What are we going to do?" Softly, someone said, "Hunger strike." Starving souls take on strength. And so the strike went on. But the guards and the warden didn't understand. They looked down at us as if we were mad—warily, from faraway.

"What do you want this time?"

"We want to be happy. We'd like for cultural programs to be instated in the prison, so we don't leave this place any dumber than when we came. We could organize concerts, go to the theatre, assemble orchestras with prison guards as musicians."

I can imagine the Sing Sing prison band playing at the Théâtre des Nations one day. The choir of guards singing like angels.

Shooting Stars

On July 24, 1971, at nine in the morning, the police showed up at my friend Anna-Maria's house. I was still asleep.

I was in Rome for a job. I had just finished working on a film by a young Italian director, Franco Brocani, about the myth of the necropolis throughout history. I played Attila, entering decadent Rome, where he was taken to a crypt in the hidden necropolis and initiated by Montezuma, the last of the Aztec emperors. In the crypt, I was undressed, then wrapped in a coat of bloody wool. An eagle was lowered onto my head and I strangled it immediately. Then I walked towards my family's tomb, at which I found a bow and arrow, as well as a white horse awaiting my arrival. I mounted it and yelled, "Horse, bring me to the hidden cities! There I can join my brothers and release them from the weight that bears down upon our shoulders, and finally liberate men from their misery!" Then the horse galloped across the studio. It's a flash, a very short scene, a prophetic parable about the fall of imperialism. Later I would indeed enter the underground church, and I would reunite with my trapped brothers.

As soon as my son Balthazar opened the door, the apartment was invaded by cops, and they tore the place apart.

"The neighbors complained," an officer said to Anna-Maria. "We are here to search the apartment."

* * *

I had also come to Rome to reflect upon the meaning of Christianity.

I always thought that in order to be an actor, one must answer to some higher order, to a rule of life and thought, a quasi-religious asceticism. I wanted to rediscover the sacred, as in Mystery plays, which were the first theatrical representations. And then introduce this sanctity to an audience awaiting revelation.

I wanted to try to find both the most mysterious and the most radiant things in life. I wanted to participate in performances that would liberate and illuminate people, rid them of their anguish, and alleviate the guilt that afflicts most of us.

This is how I imagine dramatic artists from the Middle Ages, whose mission was to communicate through their performance: they became so wise, so revolutionary, that the Church no longer had any direct power over them.

These artists restored intelligence to the people, so the Church excommunicated them. The same thing happened with America's hippies: those young people who preached ideals of love and peace, of creation and beauty, yet were deemed dangerous by American society to its "order." The very order of a society built on violence and fear, where people shut themselves in their homes every night at nine, curled around their wives and children, a gun behind the door. The goal was to stop light from shining and spreading. This is what the Manson murders did: they halted this transformation, making Americans hate each other and become the instruments of a new generation's death. One must understand that it is well within the powers of the State apparatus to perform the most terrifying provocations of hate and destruction. And if we know that, we must try to disrupt such provocations across all levels of power, from politics to journalism or art.

We must fight for our lives.

For nearly eighteen months, I had the time to confront this question from every angle: why did the cops knock on Anna-Maria's door that summer's day?

It had already been some time since anarchist Pietro Valpreda was imprisoned, almost as long as we'd been sure he was innocent. The media had exaggerated the story because the State needed a diversion, something that turned people's attention to a story that appeared threatening to the criminal justice system. It was a story that stirred up public sentiment to such an extent that people didn't have the mind to sniff out all the corruption and lies. People immediately turned their attention towards these strange, long-haired, filthy men, who refused to work and instead took drugs—hippies, new Jews. A piece of meat thrown into the lion's cage. What had I done in Rome to merit the police's attention? I'd worked a lot, acted in multiple films back-to-back, delved into various projects; otherwise, I was pretty isolated. My room was my refuge.

I didn't like Rome's "café society." For artists, Rome was a village where gossip drained all of one's energies. All who roamed this little world—actors, journalists, filmmakers, painters—were incredibly kind, and would welcome you with open arms. But it wasn't long before you realized that this world was utterly folded into itself, existing in a vacuum. They were, and they probably knew this, completely inept, useless, "luxurious." They ended up forming a sort of caste, with their privileges (money, the protection of the powerful) and their rituals: a permanent spot at Rosati's terrace on the Piazza del Popolo, as well as the nightly escapade to Trastevere, where they could see real people from a little closer up. It was a caste whose members spent most of their time entertaining, showing themselves off, entangling and disentangling and colluding with one another in an endless cycle. They didn't work for the good of the people—more than anything, they worked for themselves in order to reinforce their own egotistical pleasures. Perhaps this came from a lack of imagination, despite their fame and power, or maybe because they'd grown disillusioned. They stopped fighting because the complexity of Italy's problems was beyond them. They preferred to live and let live, to watch their own die among them and let the rest croak somewhere else. They lived in Rome, the Eternal City, which is like an open grave.

They waited for evening, at which point they would meet up with one another; for them, day was only preparation for night. I think of the peasant from the nearby countryside who works the land all day, the soil hardened by the sun. Once night falls, he returns to his home, lights a fire, and watches the flames rise.

* * *

Perhaps I puzzled the police simply by not entering into that world, not playing the "star" with a luxury car and a little courtyard, by chatting with Travestere's hippies and workers instead of the Rosati regulars.

I like the Italian people, poor people, those who toil away like beasts in order to provide for their huge families. They know a lot about life, so much more than people think. They know that the system makes them slaves, but they are full of hope and energy. They are Italy's true strength.

And of course, I had a beard, long hair, and the reputation of a hash smoker—without enough powerful protectors to let me carry on in peace.

It didn't take long for the cops to find what they were looking for. Anna-Maria, my shooting star, was taken in. They wanted to take me, too, but I couldn't leave Balthazar, who had become upset. So they let him come with me.

* * *

Here I return to the peasant who, without ever really knowing it, sows the earth and works for future generations—for the continuation of the world. His wheat or corn is already an idea, the mysterious power of truth. Every being on this planet carries within him a knowledge, and it is his duty to make this knowledge sprout across the entire earth. For me, life is a serious thing. It doesn't last very long—thirty years, forty years, fifty years. Over the course of fifty years, you must do your part in this world. And even if the peasant thinks his part is small, caring for his wife and children in peace, he is still creating for others. People don't work for posterity, they work to live. But the future of the world is already present in this work.

I hadn't truly understood this until I was in prison, when I saw all these imprisoned energies crowded together, compressed to the point of bursting, and forgotten, made unproductive. All that untended land. The youth of Rome's working-class neighborhoods, whom I'd seen with their families or at work, were locked up for almost nothing—usually it was for some petty theft because they'd lost their job. I watched them go in circles for hours, yelling in the middle of the courtyard just to let off steam.

In Italy, prisons are full because there isn't enough work for all the sons of the South who go North once a year to seek their fortune. Prisons help to absorb Southern Italy's unemployment and underdevelopment. At least twenty percent of prisoners are "travelers," migrants ambling from prison to prison because there's nothing better to do. They can't leave the country because they don't have enough money to emigrate, or because they don't have enough friends in France, Switzerland, or Germany; they get bored and start to crave excitement, so they resort to stealing from a bank, a wallet, or the till of a convenience store, and they are caught right away.

According to the logic of the system, they leave the South of their youth, after which they find no work, are forced to steal, and ultimately end up in prison. The economic advantage is twofold: this reduces the unemployment rate and bolsters the prison industry, supporting prison suppliers as well as judicial and police apparatuses. And the political advantage is to justify the perpetual mobilization of a powerful police force, the swelling of their staff, and the improvement of their repressive equipment. To justify a militia that is primed to silence any rumblings of revolutionary movement.

* * *

Balthazar didn't like the police.

"I want guns to kill the police!"

The lawyer tried to console him, and the commissioner got involved. Balthazar did not want to leave with the lawyer.

This is what they did to my son: they lied to him. They taught him hate and anger. They told him his father was guilty, yet they also said it was no big deal, he would see his father again soon. These are the kinds of lies cops feel compelled to tell when they are faced with a mystery beyond their comprehension: a child.

What did their mothers teach them? Italian mothers are wonderful. They are the she-wolves of Rome. They'd fight tooth and nail to defend their husbands and children. Family. These women know that their husbands will sometimes sleep with a whore, but that they will come back. Otherwise they'll tear apart what they once defended with the same rage. They go mad. In Italian prisons, there are hundreds of Medeas. One of them killed her three sons because her husband left her for another woman. Another girl had a lover who'd promised marriage, yet marriage never came. Then one day she decided to kill him, just like that, bang!—killing the two children she had with him, too. These shooting stars don't understand compromise: they go all in, and if their dream collapses, they make everything go up in flames. Women can burn—they are fertile. Earth can be covered in ashes. Women, women, sacred land of my birth. Men are nothing but trouble.

Balthazar was perfect. There were at least fifteen cops around, negotiating with him, flashing scary smiles. But no matter how harmless they wanted to appear, their tone wasn't right. Balthazar repeated, stubbornly, "I want guns to kill the police!" I hugged him. Go ahead, son!

The Queen of the Heavens

The prison system is the total negation of the human being.

It denies life to man, sending him back to the womb, floating in fetal form, so it can convert him into a right-minded machine.

Society uses the prisoner like fuel. Like coal in society's furnace, the prisoner is used to put more pressure on free men, who are thus made aware that they must protect their own freedom, property, and comfort. Because they forget. They forget that men die every day in the State's furnaces, in prisons throughout all the world—these men die in order for love, fraternity, and collective creation to thrive somewhere else. Prisoners are on the frontline in the fight against all wielders of power, money, culture. Inside their cells, in the depths of their misery, prisoners bear witness. They are fighting for life.

I've gone through all of society's repressive systems: correctional facilities, juvenile detention centers, asylums, criminal facilities, and now, to round it all off, prisons. I've heard so many stifled voices over the years, and all of them speak on behalf of what is true and just in this world. These voices demand that the imprisoned man be given the possibility to create, to reinvent himself; to be reborn, upon his "liberation," into a world of love and brotherhood. Because today the man who leaves prison is painstakingly contrived to end up there again.

He returns to this site of terror that has become his "home," and the saddest thing is that he ends up feeling comfortable in this house of horrors. Prisons breed criminals just as universities breed scholars, and art schools breed artists.

If only those condemned by the system were offered, at the very least, the means to emerge from its depths.

It was the condemned who taught me what innocence was.

I entered Regina Coeli with peace of mind, as if I were going on a stroll with some friends. Had I ended up believing the same tales that the police had told Balthazar to calm him down? I told myself that all I had to do was wait until the trial, and that the trial would happen soon because there was hardly anything to be investigated. The case was simple.

Regina Coeli was the prison for Rome's lower classes, the inevitable, unlucky home for the poor and weak, those unable to survive off the crumbs of the Roman feast. The prison is as old as the city, its black rock worn down by a hundred generations of entrapment. We were just as oppressed by its walls as we were by the rocks that formed them. A city prison is made up of the city itself, from its stones to its men. And like the city, a prison has its own traffic patterns, scandals, classes and castes, masters and slaves. Even though its walls are so thick, its bars and doors so numerous, the prison still courses with the life of a city—its sounds, smells, even its sights.

There were no windows at Regina Coeli. The cells—or rather the holes in the wall—were lit only through the "wolves' mouths," narrow openings that revealed a small piece of sky. But from the inner courtyard you could glimpse, just across the way, a city terrace where fiancés and prisoners' whores would come naked every Saturday, which provided some consolation for us prisoners. During this authorized forty-minute walk, friends, families, and even journalists would look at us and shout out the world news, delights and conflicts alike: how the country was doing, news of prison reforms, how the newborn was faring. This is how I saw, in the newspapers that secretly circulated, images of myself pacing in the courtyard.

The censorship was severe at Regina Coeli. An underground newspaper was distributed among prisoners. Without it, we wouldn't have gotten any news—not about politics, nor what was really happening in Italian or French prisons. But we knew. At Regina Coeli, as in all the prisons of the world, the game of telephone worked marvelously. And there was the underground press, the underground postal service. Thank goodness for these operations, because letters that went through the official route either didn't arrive or never left. And if our letters managed to make it out, they did so in shreds.

I am convinced that my mail was photocopied in full, and that in some criminal psychology laboratory, someone was analyzing who I was and what I did: what my political and sexual ideas were, if I jerked off three times a day, what influence I could possibly have had on my neighbors, if I was harmful or contagious.

Guys who were surely very serious and bedecked with diplomas were working on this all day. It was a task of the highest importance—what if I was beyond repair? Well, the employment crisis had to be solved, work had to be given to all these young people fresh out of university; it was important to box them in as quickly as possible, to force them into the system before they had time to really think about the system itself. Prisoners are pretty useful in this way: they provide work for thousands of people.

Regina Coeli's ten buildings were designed to house 1,500 prisoners; they now house more than 3,000. The system is logical in itself. Three thousand prisoners, plus the additional "services": administrators, wardens, guards, kitchen workers, suppliers, psychologists, chaplains, and I must be forgetting some. A prison is not made solely of prisoners. Just as it's not made *for* prisoners.

* * *

I stayed at Regina Coeli for a little more than eight months—until my trial, that is, which they were in no hurry to begin. Eight months of "preventive" detention that was based on mere suspicion, as well as the "strong conviction" of the judge and the police, because those who are suspected of being "junkies" are targets of very specific guidelines. For example, no one even considers sending them off to detox in a hospital. Prison's cure is what they need, and they need it now. They don't have the right to provisional freedom. Preventive detention is the law. Roman prisons are full of young people from all countries, of all races, who were deemed irrevocably criminal because they were found smoking a joint in front of Piazza di Spagna or at Trinità dei Monti. And I'm telling you, these boys will never know peace again. All it takes is one suspicion, a baseless accusation, for a police report to land on the desk of the investigating judge, and for this judge to call for handcuffs—preventive detention. Months of hell for a cigarette. And maybe all for nothing, if the jury decides to acquit. Lives wasted. That's way more dangerous than a little grass.

The very beginning, those first moments in prison are the same for everyone. It begins with the slam of the cell door that closes in on you, and you stay there, unmoving, frozen, but your heart is racing. And it's true that you can hear the beating of your own heart. At first, your mind is blank. It's impossible to string your thoughts together. You breathe—or rather, you begin to breathe again. And then your eyes focus on a point in the wall. There, right in front of you. Why there? Maybe it's a scuff on the stone, a crack, a crevice. A sloppy drawing done by one of your predecessors, an ass or a pair of tits. You think, *It's been there for years.* How many years? Two, ten, twenty? Another thought: *How many years will it be for me?* Two, ten, twenty? No, that's absurd! You wake up from this fleeting nightmare. You were falling fast, plummeting from the sky. And then it's over, it goes away. They won't just leave you here. Everything becomes instinct—your mind defends itself, defends you. You must survive, you must hope. You repeat to yourself, *It's the others who die here, not me.* And you begin to understand that you are entering into a fight against yourself.

Like all the other prisoners, I feasted not on the prison's disgusting soup, but on the sweetest of illusions. Upon hearing the slightest sound in the corridor, for every squeal of the gates, we told ourselves, "That's it, that's for me, they're coming to get me out of here." For every shattered hope, we believed this less and less, yet we forced ourselves to sustain the dream, to make-believe in the charade of a happy ending.

We would make up anything: there will be a pardon, they will change the law, important people are moving mountains to get me out of here. Even as we were telling ourselves these stories, we knew that they were just that—stories. We went on like this for a few days, maybe a week. I'd read somewhere that Giovanni Leone, the president of the Italian Republic, had been a lawyer, and I thought, this is someone who has the power, who understands the reality of prisons, he's going to do something, etc. But eventually we would let go of these shaky lifelines.

I lasted longer than the others. For two weeks I dreamt up the impossible. The problem is that you don't know the date of your trial. The entire system relies on this uncertainty—it could be tomorrow, in a month, in a year, you will never know, not during your first few days, nor even the first few weeks of your imprisonment. And this is why despite everything else, despite the days followed by yet more days, you hope, and you wear yourself out with this hope. I knew I was innocent, but I also knew that I was entering prison like an astronaut embarking upon an unknown world, unsure whether I'd ever find home again. If you know that you have to wait two, five, or ten years, you can let go of your soul and wait in peace. But you're waiting for your trial. And I'm telling you, this wait is designed to drive you mad.

I remember the words I whispered to a shooting star: *Balance and imbalance break the harmony of hope. I remain alone in darkness, waiting for tomorrow to bring something new, but my mind is tired of wanting the same thing, and the cycle continues like a slow death because I know nothing will happen tomorrow. Justice is long and grueling, and even if my innocence is eventually proven, it will leave prison in pieces.*

Madness opens its arms to you once you begin to understand that it could be months, or an eternity, before someone looks at your file. This depends on luck, on who will want (or not want) to hear your mute grievances. It depends too much on an unknown that you can neither predict nor control. This is an injustice, a repressive tactic that goes beyond your imprisonment and your everyday suffering inside the cell. This strategy is more refined than you could ever imagine.

I don't think I uttered a single word for two months. Like all prisoners, I had the right to see my lawyer. But at Regina Coeli, no one could enter the cells; no one, not even the lawyers, breached the intimate body of the prison. There was a room where the swarm of prisoners spoke to the swarm of lawyers. For two months, I refused to see them. In any case, they didn't know any more than I did about the date of the trial, and I preferred my stories to theirs. Having already been cut off from the world, I cut myself off from the prison itself. But it wasn't only out of despair. In the most extreme solitude, the soul steels itself for battle. The worst was yet to come.

It was ultimately to save myself that I retreated. Like the swimmer who, caught suddenly in a whirlpool, has only one way out: to sink passively to the bottom and push himself up to the surface.

After the silence, after the isolation, after weeks in a vegetative state, rebellion took hold. I found the strength to revolt. The only weapon available to a prisoner is himself, his body. I refused to eat, I sent back full trays to the kitchen, many times, many days in a row.

The warden was moved by this. Hunger strikes—this violence enacted by the weak—hit a sensitive spot for the bourgeois: it reveals their shame in eating like princes among the poor. He asked me what was wrong. What was wrong? He was the first to know. I asked that they change the rules of the prison, whose only purpose was apparently the prisoners' complete annihilation. I asked for a lot of things.

You know what happened next? I was deemed a dangerous threat to the prison's tranquility. Some tranquility that was. I had known solitude, and now I was going to get to know solitary. Five days in the pound. Five days wouldn't seem so long if you had enough air to breathe, if daylight came from more than just a slit in the wall, if the water you drank and the water you bathed in didn't come from the same source.

And if you were still entertaining any doubts, now everything becomes clear: you understand your fated role in this prison. You are here to serve as an example. You are here so that your imprisonment isn't entirely useless, so it can help others—both on the inside and on the outside—open their eyes to what prisons really are and to what one can do, what one must do, to salvage prisoners' humanity before it is destroyed.

Men, what are your prisons? Concentration camps, endless hells burning next door. No one will hold out their hand to help the prisoner bear his fate, no one will stop him from going lower than an animal, they will never help him prepare for the moment when he gets to return to his life. Do you know that keeping a man trapped in a cell twenty-two hours out of twenty-four is tantamount to killing him? Slowly, deliberately. Every man carries the world within him, but the prisoner's world is tragically waned by the four walls of his cell, the four steps of his walk, and the nothingness that engulfs him. Repression targets not only his past, his criminal acts, but the soul itself, which becomes dazed and destroyed. The killer has killed another person. Must he be punished? Of course. But if his freedom is withheld, one should strive to give him a new conscience. Otherwise, better to put him to death right away.

* * *

I saw some terrible things at Regina Coeli, but also some outstanding men.

A little before Christmas it got very cold in Rome, and even colder at Regina Coeli where the cells weren't heated. I remember sending a few desperate letters to my mother, asking her to knit me some wool sweaters and socks. I talked as much as I could to anyone who was willing to listen to me and explain the prison's mysteries, no matter whether it was a prisoner, priest, or guard.

The system fears the energy of the masses. The system is compelled either to block it or channel it elsewhere, to try to convert a creative force into a repressive one, at all costs. Recruiter sergeants go looking for the most frustrated men, the rawest in Italy, the idle sons from the South or the children of the mountains, from Adige or Abruzzo, twenty-year-olds who have never seen a city, who can't read or write. The recruiter sergeants make the rounds of the countryside. They say to the boys, "Come to Rome, to Milan, where there are the loveliest girls in all the country, and there are cinemas, we will guarantee you a fabulous career, you will make 180,000 lire a month." There are a hundred, two hundred, a thousand of them who leave their farms and their mammas, who come down from the mountains at the end of every summer. Selections are made, tests are administered, and about half of them make it through. They are educated, taught to read and write. Then they are forced to sign an employment contract to be in the *celeri* or to be a prison guard. They are taught to harm. They are given amphetamines before protests. The same thing happened with the troops of men who, as soon as they landed in Algeria, were handed a gun and told, "The Arabs want to kill you—defend yourself." They are overseen by experienced veterans, military men, specialists of repression and propaganda. They are lured in by promotions. If they get married, they are given 100,000 lire, 120,000 for the first born, and so on.

And this is how, at just twenty-five years old, they end up in prison, guarding men who are ultimately just like them, children from the South or the mountains, their brothers.

When prisoners revolt, when there are too many complaints, a hundred guards are poised to take to their rifles and batons and slaughter you if you don't wait patiently for the Minister's response to your demands. And if the Minister says no and you continue to insist, there are a hundred readymade men trained to beat you to a pulp until you shrink under their power.

Day after day, their supervisors repeated to the mountain men that we were dangerous, fundamentally evil, and that we were primed to kill their wives and their children, too; they were told that we were lost causes who only understood the language of violence. So they distrusted us and knocked us around. A prison's harmony relies on the balance of fear. You fear the guards and they fear you. You may be tempted to break this vicious cycle of distrust and retaliation. Sometimes all it takes is a few words, or a single look, to change an order imposed by terror. The youngest guards are not yet rooted in—or rotted by—the system and haven't yet grasped that all they've been told are myths. Or that they, too, have been tricked. They don't understand that the prisoners they monitor are just people who, instead of being exploited by the State or their bosses, took life by the balls, found some friends, and held up a bank—because banks steal from the people.

Sometimes all you have to do is speak the truth to whomever is in front of you, even if he is in uniform, because this truth can work to undermine the architecture of false values that have been put in his head.

There were guards in their early twenties who would visit me in my cell. They would ask, "You're Pierre Clémenti?"

"Yeah, that's me. Pierre Clémenti."

"Ah! I've seen you in *Belle de Jour* and *Benjamin*. Why are you here?"

"Drugs."

"Italian law is severe when it comes to drugs," one of them tells me.

"Yes, it's very strict," I said. "How old are you?"

"Twenty-two."

"Do you know that you're going to stay in this prison for another twenty-five years?"

"What do you mean?"

"I'm privileged, maybe I'll do two or three years, but after that I'll be free. But you'll be here for twenty-five years."

"How's that?"

"You have chosen a career. Maybe in twenty-five years, you'll be chief guard."

"No, no, I don't want to be here for twenty-five years!"

"Then what are you going to do?"

"It's really hard to find work around here, you know. My contract is for three years."

"After three years, get out of here, beat it," I told him. "Take a boat, go on a trip, don't waste your youth in prison. It's fine if you do a year or two on the inside, that way you'll get to know your brothers who have been accused of being irredeemable. But you ought to hold on to them, talk to them, and never forget that you're a man before you're a uniform, and then get the hell out of here, live your life, go abroad, roam across the world and create what you want to create."

Around Christmas, four young guards left with doctor's notes that stated they were "unable to adapt to the prison environment." They never came back. One of them became a ship's steward, and I don't know what happened to the others. We can count on the mountain men—they are in good health, and they don't need a union to understand that their job is shit.

Guards escaped from Rebibbia, too. The management installed indoor cameras so they could watch their own guards. This is proof that they were even more imprisoned than we were.

After the second revolt, the management gave the order to kill those suspected of having spearheaded it, and of the fifty guards ordered to beat up prisoners with lead pipes, three refused. "I came here to be a keyholder, to watch over the inmates, not to hit them, not to treat them like dogs." The military court sentenced them to six months of prison for insubordination. Six months on the other side of the door. And we witnessed an assembly of guards call for the freedom of their imprisoned comrades.

Many guards began to understand that they didn't have to beat up the prisoners. Prisoners never hit first, or if they do, it's because they're provoked to violence as legitimate defense.

A horrible story helped reveal the truth, casting a shadow over the guards. A prisoner had slapped a guard who was insulting him. The guard didn't react. But that night, the guard and four of his friends broke into the guy's cell. They rolled him up with his bedsheet. They hit him all over, perhaps without aiming, or perhaps knowing exactly where they were hitting. The prisoner was castrated.

Word gets around pretty fast in prison. The next day, everyone knew. Winds whispered, doors closed, silences lingered. The guards felt alone and trembled in fear. The inmates' mute rage was a terrifying force, and transformed the guards into distraught beasts who paced in circles around the hallways for hours on end. The guards sought out prisoners' gazes, hoping to find some hatred there. But they found only empty eyes. The repressive, enormous machine had been stopped, the ark was drifting away, and the absurdity of all gestures, schedules, and rules suddenly became clear. We all understood the profound, desperate uselessness of this circus. I think the majority of the guards would prefer to die underground. As fragile and suppressed as a prison is, there's still some life there. But it can only survive through the bond that ultimately unites the prisoners with the guards. If the stubborn child no longer respects the rules of the game, the game is over.

I learned to tell the difference between real guards and the people who hide behind the scenes—the administrators, who never dare to climb the iron stairs or walk through the corridors. Each prison employs a comfortable bureaucratic apparatus composed of petty bosses who control everything. What an exhilarating feeling of power for a superintendent to decide, in the hideout of his office, the menu for the six thousand meals that are served each day. What exhilarating, bountiful power. The real deals aren't done with the guards, who can be bought easily and cheaply. The big sums are traded under the table, within the upper administration. The Italian State allocates the prison management 7,000 lire per day, per prisoner. It was one of our favorite games to calculate how much we were really costing the prison. Taking the prices used in the Roman markets as your starting point—notwithstanding the discounts and tips that go to the big buyers, as well as the terrible quality of the food—you're at 2,000 maximum. Five thousand was missing, lost somewhere along the way. One million five hundred thousand lire per day for Regina Coeli alone. Prisoners are good business! Directly or indirectly, prisoners feed more parasites than prisons could ever hold.

* * *

None of the prisoners work. Most of them, who are in total misery, would actually prefer some kind of work program, through which they could make about 15,000 lire a month. The prison's few essential jobs are in the kitchens, sanitation crews, and infirmaries, and these jobs are for the longtimers, or for those who will become longtimers. I knew an old professor who had been there for twenty-five years. Twenty-five years is the maximum penalty (you cannot be condemned to life in prison in Italy), but it's still well beyond the time that a human being can stand being in prison. He was a broken man, he could hardly walk, but he would have died if it hadn't been for his job in the infirmary. He accompanied the nurse during her morning and evening rounds, dragging his feet but nonetheless proud of his role that almost exclusively consisted of doling out pills and tranquilizers to the sick. He started to study medicine; he gave advice, explaining to prisoners why they were sick, and the official doctor did everything else. His biggest fear was that he was going to leave soon. His twenty-five years were almost over.

"You're going to leave, doc?"

"Yes, but what am I going to do? After twenty-five years!"

"You'll live in the countryside, you can fish!"

"I fished when I was young, I caught these enormous carps…"

I saw prisoners who were in anguish at the prospect of their freedom. Like the prisoner who, on the morning of his execution, dreads the dawn. A guard comes to get you. You're led to the warden's office. You already know that it's the end and it's the beginning. You get a little speech from the warden. They hope never to see you again, they wish happiness to your family and in your work, and so on. You are only half listening. What family? What work? What are my wife's breasts like these days? What do my children's eyes look like? Don't I stink of prison? After masturbating so much, will I still be able to make love to the woman who may someday be my wife? Will I recognize the street, or house, from which I was torn ten years ago? All the questions that you've dwelled on for ten years come back to you in a second. Your head spins, you're struck by vertigo. The warden sits you down. He knows that prisoners, barely out the door, fall into dust and fade away, devastated. They go straight from the prison to the hospital for what is sure to be a difficult recovery.

Most of them come back in no time. No one "outside" wants anything more from them. It didn't work out with the wife, with work even less. In Italy, he who leaves prison isn't marginalized like he would be in France. There is a solidarity among the people. He isn't blacklisted; in fact, friends and neighbors have a celebration on the day of his return. But as much as that's worth, there is no work to be found. It makes sense. Others have long since taken the places that he once occupied. He has forgotten his craft, if he ever had one, and he hasn't learned another. Prison is, once again, the only solution. He relapses.

At Regina Coeli, only a few prisoners had the determination, strength, and patience to study. Everyone had the time. But it takes willpower and perseverance to open a book and then finish it, take notes, take classes remotely, and also to ignore all the jokes and harassment from your neighbors and the guards. I knew one prisoner who studied Roman law for six years. He had gotten his bachelor's degree and had now become *dottore*. Surely he would be well off, once "outside." But nothing in the prison's structure was designed to help him, nor to encourage others to follow in his footsteps. There are exhausting procedures if you want to get a book that isn't part of the library's dismal catalog. Then there are questionnaires, formalities, and papers of all kinds to fill out in order to be authorized to take an exam.

During my eight months at Regina Coeli, I didn't open a single book; the only things I read were the letters that reached me. But I never stopped thinking about everything that could have been generated by these imprisoned energies, now wasted. Three thousand men sailing together for months, years, towards what *should* be their own liberation—except that they are shackled to an enforced idleness, stuck like slaves in the ship's hold, with no say whatsoever in the final destination. I knew that there were enough forces to transform an entire prison into a place of creation and research—research for the prisoners themselves, not for the psychologist-cops who condensed us into spreadsheets.

I also wrote letters to all of the stars who had shot through my life. *Françoise—I am sending you this letter through a non-censored messenger. Perhaps when you receive it I will already be declared innocent, otherwise I'll spend Christmas with my brothers here, as we struggle to overcome violence and stay awake. It is important for you to know that we are waging war here, and that the prison system is more difficult to change than the world was to create in seven days, believe me—but the energy of the masses remains alive, despite all the repression. Each of us is confined to a cage twenty-two hours a day, like a savage animal that leaves only to circle the grounds under the shadow of a whip. But we are stronger than our trainers and we will win the right to be respected...*

It was just before Christmas when my neighbor was brought in again. He'd been released just two weeks earlier. He was a young, brooding man who spoke little, I think he was Piedmontese. I never knew the reasons for his being there, and he said he was innocent, too. Two weeks before Christmas, he was pardoned. Italian prisons are emptied out at Christmastime. Thousands of prisoners are filtered back into the system, but many relapse. This one did, too, because I saw him brought back to the same cell he'd occupied for two weeks, the one just next to mine. No one knew how he'd managed to sneak in the nylon wire with which he hung himself. Hung himself badly. The wire broke, but his neck was already shattered. I heard the thud of his body hit the floor and some stray gasps. I bashed on my door like a madman. It didn't open right away. In any case, he was already dead.

A Lifeline to the Unknown

My other neighbor in the cell block was a painter. Rather, he painted.

After solitary, I'd earned the right to some respect. And in prison, the rule of thumb is that after a few months—two or three, depending on the person—the rules begin to loosen. The initial observation period—during which time you are left to wrestle with yourself, trapped in cement, sealed in silence, where experts in despair test your defenses—gives way to a calmer climate. Having undergone this initiation ritual, you're admitted into the ring of prison routine. Your status is normalized. More and more with each passing day, the tenuous link of trust connects you to the other prisoners and to the guards themselves. They know that you have passed the threshold and, barring accident, you'll drink up your dose of prison until its last drop. You now belong to this immense family, you're in solidarity with them, you won't provoke violence from those in power, and you won't betray the secrets that this family shares with you. Faces light up as you pass, you become the new bearer of confidences that have been uttered a thousand times, yet which become new again in your presence. You are hearing them for the first time. Your neighbors come to talk to you. On your walks, your companions unfurl their lives' drama before your eyes.

This walk, I must clarify, was now longer. Two hours instead of the forty minutes that were first granted—three times as many steps, more time for listening.

"There are days where I'm in a good mood, and others when I can't help but sulk. I don't know why…"

How can one answer this droning litany of daily woes?

He continued, "Perhaps it's because of sleep, the dreams I have. You know, I still dream about it sometimes…"

I don't know what dream keeps coming back to this man holding my arm in his as we round the courtyard—is it his wife, the crime that led him here, the day of his freedom?

"When you go into a bistro, you have to pay. You can't just walk off."

More than anything else, prisoners really need to talk, that's for sure. It's not enough to breathe in the air and smell the scents that waft into the prison from the city. Calls and responses are shouted across the courtyard. "How's the trial going?" "Giustizia di merda!" "And the lawyer?" "Va fare in culo l'avvocato!" Thrilled, you hear the Italian language ring with insults.

"Even if you're only having a coffee, you can't not pay—"

"You can go in a bistro and order a coffee. You look at the man having a drink next to you. You look him in the eye, and he pays for your coffee."

There was a time when I hung around Saint-Germain-des-Prés, picking up cigarette butts from the street and smoking them. One day, a guy came up to me and said, "Come with me, we need you, I'm sure you'll be perfect." I followed him into a big house where people dressed in medieval costumes were rehearsing a play. It was *Procès aux Templiers*. One of them came towards me while the rest continued to practice. He looked at me in the eyes, I looked back, and in this gaze a long friendship was born.

"What's your name?"

"Pierre Clémenti."

"I'm Jean-Pierre Kalfon. Do you want to work in theatre? Come on, I'll show you how…"

The prisoner—Giuseppe was his name, but everyone called him Pino—wouldn't believe my story. "Things like that only happen in dreams." I tried to tell him how he didn't believe enough in those around him. The world is full of unknown friends who can help you find your way. We're all born under the same sky.

That's how I became an actor. I met a stranger who told me, "Take the plunge! Go for it!" That first play made me realize that I had to become aware of my shortcomings. Voice, diction, body, movement—I realized that I had to work, and it was Jean-Pierre who gave me the strength to learn, as well as the will to take a weekly class in dramatic arts. I went to the Théâtre du Vieux-Colombier, where Dullin had reigned, then to the Théâtre National Populaire. I even went to the Conservatoire rue Blanche, but for only three weeks—it wasn't to my liking.

You need someone to take a chance on you, someone who invites you to rise up and create, who gives you the determination to seize upon something that you suspect might already exist within you, but which you lack the power to really identify. I know that there is a creator inside every man, and whether this light can shine or diminish is dependent upon those around him. Prisons are full of them—artists who don't know what to do with themselves because no one ever told them, "You're in here for five years, twenty years? Go ahead, my son, and make something of it!" Some prisoners naturally understood this, and made what they could with the materials at hand.

Their craft may seem trivial in comparison to high art, but I knew guys who collected all the matches they could find and carefully, lovingly, they made these fabulous model caravels, ships that would never sail across any sea in the world. This gesture demonstrates prisoners' creative and irrepressible power.

I knew some great artists in prison who took a year to make a painting—but why rush, anyway? No dealer was waiting for their delivery. My neighbor had been sentenced to seven years for killing his wife. When I got to know him, he had already done five. He was in a really bad state. He usually didn't talk to anyone, but one day he came to see me.

"You should try to paint."

He seemed more or less insane, and all the other guys watched out for him. It was said that he cried all the time, that he couldn't handle it. He must be out by now. I hope he's okay.

"Why don't you try?" he insisted.

"Isn't it difficult?"

He was a fresco specialist and had painted the prison chapel, hoping that this work would reduce his sentence. Maybe that's why people distrusted him: everyone knew he'd do anything to leave as soon as possible. To paint, he said, all you have to do is feel. "What is beauty? In order to create a beautiful thing, you must go back to the very essence of life, to desire."

His name was Raphaël.

I started to paint the scene of a circus I'd seen as a child, and I tried to render everything that the eyes of childhood allowed me to see. The sparkling lights and fierce colors—the same things that prison robs from you. The circus was set up near the village where we lived, and our uncles brought me and my brother Maurice there. I must have been about seven or so. I really wrestled with this first canvas, clinging to it as though it were a lifeline. I could no longer see the world, so now I would paint it. I became the kind of desperate onlooker who I often think about when I'm acting in a play or in a film: the audience member who is here by chance, just so he can get away. And through the creative act in which you participate, you can actually address him, and you can throw him a lifeline that might help him save himself.

The circus was like a communion. Joy and recklessness rose up inside me when I painted, just as they did when we went with our uncles to the forest of cork oaks, looking for mushrooms, or when we spent the whole day in the hills, pulling up heather that our uncles would then sell at the factory. That evening, drunk on fresh air and exhausted from the day, we sat down at a common table, devouring the soup that the aunts had kept warm in the hearth all day, and listened to our grandfather who always had a Corsican legend to tell.

The painter was right: all you had to do was feel. And perhaps there is no better place to feel than the prison cell. Cut off from the outside world, you open yourself up to the other world of your memories, and spend hours looking deep within yourself, walking towards the horizon that is your childhood. Or towards a form of madness, if the waves of memory rise and drown you. This is how prison both endangers and seduces you: it's a place where fantasy runs wild.

I painted like a child in a style that could be called "naïve," and my mentor smiled when I told him that I didn't know how or where to begin a painting. "You paint everything all at once," he said. And I did just that, because the impressions and images behind my paintings were so vivid in my memory. On an uneven plywood rectangle, on a coarse box, with paintbrushes and schoolboy colors, the world entered the prison, everything all at once. And with each naive image, I made a window through the walls.

The Father's Judgment

At this point I was seeing my lawyers every week. My manager at the William Morris Agency had handled my situation pretty well: I had two lawyers, Filippo Ungaro and Paolo Appella. That's why I was in a somewhat privileged position at Regina Coeli. Most prisoners could only ever expect a state-appointed attorney who, while surely capable of doing his job, nonetheless bore less weight in the eyes of the prosecutors than the lawyers I could afford. This is how justice, despite its universally lauded equality, inevitably skews towards the rich at the expense of the poor.

The investigation was nearly finished, the lawyers confidently declared. "You know, the judge can attach his name to a 'first' in jurisprudence. This has never happened before. That counts for a lot."

I had already met the judge three times during interrogations and face-to-face meetings. And three times I restated my ignorance, my innocence. I could see that he didn't really know how to deal with me. He talked to me as if I were a child, with a kind of forced softness. "Monsieur Clémenti, how can that be possible? You'd been living in this apartment for six months and yet you didn't know there were drugs inside?" He insisted, warily, "But

they're saying you take drugs?" He made an effort not to seem aggressive.
"I don't take drugs."
"But you smoke?"
"Sure, I smoke. I smoke cigarettes."

* * *

The lawyers had opened a dispute over legal procedure, which was essentially a fight about principles. It so happened that a certain law, which had been passed for a year at that point, had never been put into action: it required that the police perform interrogations and searches only in the presence of the defendant's attorney. Obviously, that's not how things played out on Via dei Banchi Vecchi at Anna-Maria's apartment. The very basis of the investigation was null. The police didn't respect the law. And my lawyers tried their best to remind the judge and the public of this.

In your every encounter with the judge, you feel the circle closing in on you. All your past exploits end up in your file.

Except it's not really your story. At most, it's the story of your chains. I am a different person than the one determined, described, and defined by the reports.

You object—it simply can't be that the conviction they are threatening you with is already decided based on your official record, your tribulations in rehabilitation centers, asylums, and "homes." You know that your life cannot be reduced to this list that gets longer every time someone reads it to you. But you created something, too. Every time you were locked up, you got out, you struggled, and you made it through. "But none of this is in my file, Your Honor. You're missing all the good." What's essential is always missing from the file that trails you. "But you can't deny that you're a regular at some of these places, Monsieur Clémenti! How do you explain that?" And with the gracious smile of someone who is quick to forgive, he added, "I want to believe you."

* * *

The judge postponed the lawyers' appeal. The machine wouldn't be stopped, the trial would go on.

"But where is the proof, Your Honor? There are only suspicions."

This repressive system never did me any favors. I often wound up in a cage at the Saint-Germain police station, simply because a police car passed me in the street. I had long hair, could hardly stand up straight, and certainly couldn't make a run for it. I was broke, and often went two weeks with next to no food. When you've gone two weeks without nourishing your body and you roam the streets, you move inside an unbelievable light: the soul of life is around you, and you no longer need to curb your desire to eat because the simple fact of continuing to live by drinking some fountain water is enough to sustain your spirit. You float, blinded by the light, and you fall down on the pavement in illumination as others fall out of weakness.

Society condemned me every chance it got. The first revolt against imposed order leads to more punishment that is inevitably answered by yet more revolt. Condemned for having revolted, and condemned to revolt again.

Maybe this is all because I was born out of wedlock. I don't remember having known my father. I heard he was killed in the war some months after my birth, and he was rarely mentioned in my mother's family (he hadn't married her). The judge was right to insist upon what he called my "antecedents": "born of an unknown father," "illegitimate son." From the moment of my birth, I have been moored to transgression.

* * *

At Regina Coeli I met Charlie, a Frenchman, who got two years for smoking a joint. He was a really good guy. An orphan, parents nowhere to be found, social assistance, juvenile detention, asylums, La Santé Prison, Fresnes Prison—the whole gamut. He washed the prison's windows and was much respected among his fellow prisoners. He would tell them everything, because he wasn't afraid of the truth. He was very violent and extremely nervous, but was not entirely distrusted because he had experience. He reached the end of his time three weeks before my trial. He said, laughing, "I'm going to get locked up again, that's for sure. They'll never be able to leave me alone. I have too much baggage."

The chaplain summoned him the night before his release. He knew that without money, Charlie had no chance of making it, so he gave him twenty thousand lire. It was for travel and for food on the road. Twenty thousand isn't much, but it's enough for you to buy some pipes, eat a good meal, sleep in a hotel, and eventually find a friend who will open their door for you.

He got as far as Amsterdam and he's still there. I think he's doing well, he's working, he's found his star. He sent me some postcards while I was at Rebibbia with some scribbled words, as plainspoken as usual: "I think I'm really happy. I have rediscovered the meaning of life. You wanna know what it is? Having someone next to you who lights you up, having a job that allows you to eat, and to be a slave no more…"

All my life, I've made an effort to identify my father with society, with the community of men. But the society I had to deal with was full of cops and judges. My father might as well be Buddha!

Green Faces

On February 17, 1972, six months and three weeks after my arrest, I was taken from Regina Coeli and shoved between two officers for a day of crowds, speeches, and vertigo.

The sudden break from the prison's daily cycle was dizzying; I had been pulled from my cell at eight in the morning to be driven to court. Then there's the wait—in the hallways, the doorways, the car. I had been preparing for this event for so long: I had conferred with the lawyers, hypothesized my chances, solidified my statements. On this first outing, you think this is the first step towards your release, an early taste of freedom that—and you're sure of this—will be declared during the hearing.

But anything you think up to reassure yourself will end up worrying you even more, and from the cell to the courtroom the contrast is so stark, the transition so brief, that when you finally walk up the four wooden steps leading to the bench, you stumble. You blow your entrance onto the stage, but only in your eyes. Because the audience sees this failure as the perfect representation of your role as the accused: the court is a drama in which each person is supposed to stay in character, and the mise-en-scène is not subject to change.

* * *

"May the defendant rise."

Already you can't remember your lines. My familiarity with the stage did nothing to help me: I was shaking, not even daring to open my eyes. The crowd was the same—curious and complicit, the usual mix of friends and strangers—but this was an altogether different experience than the bliss of the *café-théâtres*. Eventually I looked out at the room. In the car, as we were driving, it took a while for my eyes to get used to the movement of the streets. And it required yet more time to really let the images of the crowd sink in, to identify familiar faces that I'd so yearned to see again and which now I struggled to recognize.

"Lù Leone, my Roman mother in film, you who welcomed Balthazar into your home when he lost his dad. Hello all, dear friends, who have come to see me…"

Filmmakers, actors, and journalists also came. The lawyer said, "You'll see, this will be an important trial." He took attendance, counted heads. The math was simple. The solidarity of famous names from cinema and the press, flashing cameras, petitions passed around the lobby—all of this put the judges in the position of being judged themselves.

"Please state your name."

"Pierre Clémenti, born on September 28, 1942 in the 14th arrondissement of Paris, at six in the morning…"

Later my friends will tell me how frightening I looked when I got up to answer the questions from the presiding judge. Yet I stood up straight, head high. But I was white as a sheet, near death, with hollowed cheeks and sunken eyes.

"According to Law 1041, passed on October 22, 1954, you are hereby accused of the possession and use of narcotics, the police report having established that…"

I stopped listening. I knew this part by heart. And I knew

what answers to give. I wanted to turn towards Anna-Maria, who was seated further down from me on the same bench. But I didn't have the strength. I also wanted to take advantage of the slightly perverse pleasure I'd promised myself: to be a spectator to my own trial, to assess the arguments and their rebuttals, to regard the sweeping declarations and theatrical gestures as if it were all about somebody else. I couldn't do it. I simply couldn't stay in Courtroom No. 4 and obey the ritual commands.

"You may be seated."

* * *

After returning to my cell that evening, I wrote: *Tenderness, calm, the freedom to dream, I met my brothers at the dead end where grief devours the days of the convicted; I roamed from one principle to the next; I cherished birth, love, destiny, bedrooms, street sounds. The sea rose in the distance, swelling with foam. It's there, I know, where one may find the wondrous gardens that we seeded; I found the city still but alive, I rediscovered the neon of the everyday.*

I started writing at around the same time that I was wandering the Paris streets to discover a new way of living, a new life. I'd stopped looking for work. For a year I walked around Saint-Germain with my head drooped towards the cobblestones. Saint-Germain is really a city within a city, with its populations, classes, and rituals; its arrivals and departures, the sudden and definitive disappearances of guys you'd see for months in the same spot, as well as the emergence of new faces, which, in a matter of hours, would become familiar to everyone. And at the heart of the city, in the depths of this solitude, I felt a great need to communicate something: poetry's violent desire. I wrote, yet at the same time I couldn't get through a book, it was impossible for me to concentrate on a single page, to focus my attention on a word. I was absolutely incapable of reading and perhaps it was this loss that compelled me to write.

* * *

"What do you have to say in your defense?"

I stood up again. I wanted to be there as little as possible, to shorten the great ceremony. "I confirm what I already said to the investigators. I am totally innocent of these allegations."

Then I leaned back onto my corner of the bench—too bad if I disappointed the judges and possibly the entire room, who wanted a more exciting show. The lawyers would be in charge of the rest.

* * *

I landed in Saint-Germain and barely moved after that. At that time, around '57 or '58, the Saint-Germain crowd was full of good people. These people really lived, they still had some life and warmth left in them, and they knew how to look each other in the eyes so that they really saw one another, even if they'd never exchanged words, even if they'd never met. They were wide awake to life. They understood the fragility of meaning and feelings. They held few illusions and were supportive of drifters because they kept their eyes open to the world. In their own way, they fought and built for others. I think of those among you—poets, visionaries, doctors, prophets, actors, philosophers, architects—who came quickly into my life and who are now dead, like Arthur Adamov, or are pursuing a different and perhaps less painful journey, or a more difficult one, than what they knew in Saint-Germain.

Writing, painting, and striving in my prison were ways of trying to gather these energies that time had diluted and exhausted, to resuscitate the whole of this life that was given to me, and to summon from it a force that could help my brothers and give them hope for creation.

* * *

"So you do not deny that you lived in this apartment as if it were your own?"

"Sure, but I never knew there were drugs there."

There are three judges, two men and one woman. It's the woman who really insists. My responses clearly dissatisfy her. She is relentless, determined to find me at fault—but with whose rage? I'm convinced that I must horrify her, that she's fighting as if to protect her child from the degenerate she believes me to be, in the name of all mothers who have lost faith in their sons. Woman, do not reject life, do not burden children with laws that were not made by mothers: open yourself up to tenderness.

* * *

I stayed at Regina Coeli for one week after the ruling, and I painted my trial so I could finally see the show. The podium, the courtroom, each eye of every person in the audience. Then I painted the judges: green is the color that came to their faces. Green, because they are on the fringes of life, even though they have a home and a family. Green, because they are bored to death by their wives and children. Green, because they have neither the time nor the inclination to know anything about the world—they see only files, not people. They don't even know what's happening in their own country, they don't know anything about the lives of the peasant, the factory worker, the homeless person, the whore. They know nothing but they judge anyway. The file has spoken, and for them, paper is more important than people.

* * *

It's the voice of Anna-Maria, here, right next to me, that brings me back to the room. She has risen, I see her black hair. "My statement has not changed."

"Can you explain to us how the drugs could have found their way into your furniture?"

The presiding judge won't believe us either. That would be too easy, the trial would lose its spark. The presiding judge is there to split hairs, he's the one who can't be convinced. I've known more than one of his kind, a ringleader who asks questions only when he already knows the answers. Whatever you say will confirm his conviction that you are lying. And in your answers, they're waiting for only one thing: to ensnare you even deeper in your lie. You are the lie, and they are the truth.

* * *

When I left the Montesson rehabilitation center, I had only one thing: a letter of recommendation for the Post, Telegraphs, and Telephones Employment Center. I was hired as an intern telegrapher. I biked across Paris delivering telegrams for a year and a half. Enough time for my hair to grow out.

When my hair had grown long, one concierge called me a chick. And, well, I responded! He reported me. I was reprimanded, and then a report was written up by the chief of police, whose rationale was "long hair and bohemian clothes." So I left the bike behind, and found a job as a bellman at the Hôtel le Littré.

* * *

Anna-Maria bursts into tears.

"But I've told you that my house was open to everyone, day and night. I didn't know half the people who stayed there!"

How could these judges believe in something as pure as a door that is always open and welcoming, a haven for the migrant, a light in the darkness for the wanderer? A house without locks, windows without bars, the virtue of hospitality. I imagine the judges' homes, a set of keys in their pockets, their curtains closed for fear of family secrets being swept away by the breeze.

Sleeping Beauty

Our judge was also named Anna-Maria. I'd been picturing the judge as a noble old man, a tribe elder. But she wasn't that old, and it probably wasn't that long ago that she'd nursed her child (if she had one, that is). All through the hearing I wanted her to sense my son's gaze upon her. My feeling was that a mother could never doubt innocence, and a woman who has loved could never kill youth. Look at me, woman! I'm the one who makes you a judge. Forget your widow's gown.

The prosecutor perked up. Suddenly we were plunged into the trial's melodrama—his pointed index finger, tragic tone, the automatic emotions of a stage veteran. Everything was clear to him. I'd lived at Anna-Maria's for some time, and a lot of "strange people" (these were his words) spent time there; therefore I must have known that the drugs were there. And many of my friends took drugs; therefore, I took drugs too. I was flabbergasted. I thought this was ridiculous, and that soon everyone would burst out laughing. With his hands, my lawyer communicated something like, "This won't hold up, we'll get 'em!" Then it was my lawyer's turn, he spoke for maybe an hour. I wasn't listening anymore. A single word reached me: freedom.

* * *

A woman entered, just as they do every day in every hotel. She had that fancy, long-distance traveler's perfume, furs, and trunks that weighed heavier with each step. She'd come from London and already had tickets for Milan. The names of these unknown cities filled my fantasies. Now I understand that I'd worked at post offices and at one hotel in order to be embraced, if only somewhat, by other people's journeys, to travel vicariously all over the world. My departure from the confinement of supervised facilities hadn't been enough: I needed to wander into the unknown. Traveler, I waited for you for a long time, but I was sure you would come. You didn't lock your door, either.

I helped carry her trunks up to her room. I tried to catch her gaze; I always want to see a woman's eyes. I saw a flash in them. She motioned for me to come closer. She took my hand in hers and closed my fingers around a bill. She was smiling. I left very quickly and ran away as if to escape—I'd been called down to the lobby. I didn't see her again that day. My shift ended at eight, but I didn't leave the hotel. She came down around eleven and didn't see me as she crossed the lobby; her hair was curled now, and lighter, too. She seemed younger than she had that morning. I can't remember how much longer I waited. I flipped through a book, unable to make out even a single sentence.

I didn't turn on the lights of the third-floor hallway because I knew the layout by heart. I kept still, hidden in shadow, listening for any movements or sounds from the hotel. I love hotels—the kingdom of the transient, where perpetual uncertainty soothes the vagabond. You own nothing, you have no attachments, no bed to sleep in, no paper to write on. Except for when all the windows are flung open, every apartment ends up seeming like a prison to me. Hotels induce the same kind of vertigo as the one you experience when you travel long distances, the same feeling you get when you smoke: beings and objects appear suspended in the unknown, on the brink of surprise.

* * *

A few years ago when a journalist asked me if I did drugs, I'd told her that I smoked, like everyone else, but that drugs were my enemy because they aren't a form of travel, but rather a form of imprisonment. At my trial they had interrogated a girl, Ornella, whom they'd hunted down. She was a good person. She had come to testify in my defense. But they considered her interview as incriminating evidence. She'd been troubled by my conviction; she would later attempt suicide. A suicide for a question, two years of prison for an answer.

* * *

The hotel was quiet. I approached her door, which wasn't entirely shut, and pushed it open. The unknown woman appeared to be sleeping. I hardly heard the sound of her breath, and I held my own. My eyes adjusted to the dark, but I didn't dare pass the room's threshold.

"Come here," you said to me, or perhaps I just imagined this invitation. I crossed the short distance that separated myself and the bed where you slept, where I immediately understood that you were only pretending to sleep. I wanted to end the game.

"Were you waiting for me?"

She didn't respond but turned towards me, propping herself up on one of the pillows. She turned on the bedside lamp.

"Come here so I can see you."

You took my hand and gently pulled me in.

"What would your boss say if he knew that you came into the rooms of sleeping women at night?"

I love the quiet strength in women. I love that once they have chosen a path, nothing can get in their way, just as nothing stops a shooting star.

Smiling, she said, "I don't want to know your name. I'm just in bed with a bellman." But I needed to talk to her as a son would to his mother after a long period of aimlessness. She said, laughing, "I'm fucking a bellman who is a poet…"

She wanted to give me money and I refused. "Why?" I asked. "This is already enough."

"You're being stupid. Let me buy your poems, then."

So I sold them.

With this money I was able to quit the hotel job and hold out for a few weeks, by which point a friend had helped me get hired at a stone cutting shop. It was winter, and it didn't take long for me to get frostbite on the job. Lucky for me, the workers went on strike two days later. And I never returned.

The Stone of Life

"What do you have to say for yourself?"

From where I stood, between two officers dressed like divine angels, flaming swords in hand, or when I collapsed in the street from hunger and awoke in a hospital bed between two nurses in vivid white—indeed, what did I have to say for myself? Every now and then, you must stand up for yourself with silence and say nothing before those who have come to examine and judge you. You must force them to consider who you are, your stubborn nature, so they can begin to understand that what they seek to locate in you is their own guilt, or their own innocence. In my silence, I wanted my judges to realize that I owed them nothing, that I had the same right to refusal as they did, and that we were on the same ark, the same journey. This muteness made them hear the very sound of their judgment.

"It's ludicrous to regard the person who consciously and deliberately does drugs with the same compassion one would give some wayward victim, even if they are just experimenting. It's preposterous to compare the addict to a cigarette smoker or an alcoholic. In fact, drug use does not allow for occasional, moderate, or manageable consumption because the command of narcotics is invariably immense and oppressive, even with the mildest of uses."

When the presiding judge had finished, I knew that the ruling had been decided well before the witnesses would have the chance to testify. It wasn't my trial being held here: it was a trial about drugs and addicts. It was about those who could have been or who could become addicts. Never mind, then, the moral imperative of truth or even that of individual respect, because all that matters is that your case be representative, that you resemble the composite drawing of the addict, that they look at you and see the addict embodied—it's about fitting the role. What's even worse, I think, is this: drugs are only there as a pretext, a symbol. The addict isn't the only person being targeted; it's through his image that all of society's bastards, bands of outsiders, and any others who don't conform to the norms of the moment are also targeted. And any departure from the norm is then judged and stifled.

I'd suffered through the beginning of the trial because I wanted to speak but didn't have the strength; I needed to release all the words I'd bottled up for six months, and the courtroom would be my stage. But then, when I realized why I was really there and understood the point of the trial—that by punishing me the Italian court wanted simply to make an example—I was done talking. It was better for the room to swell with silence, for the executive judges to go to the end of their task, and for everyone to see how far they dared to go. So I froze—I became a monolith, an unidentified statue fresh out of the ground; I turned to the experts interrogating me and asked them about their own origin, their own destiny. I was the stone of life when I asked them, "Why are you here? Do you know why you are doing this? Are you even alive?"

I understood that they had died from practicing justice, from being the instruments of it. There they were: a prosecutor who demanded "his" two years as if he would be humiliated by not getting them, a priestess who only celebrated life's end, and a presiding judge who was bored to death by the lawyers trying to plead your case. I admired the lawyers for trying to revive these zombies, for relentlessly trying to breathe some life and warmth into them, although the judges are bored out of their minds. For them, the fate of the case has been sealed since the very beginning; they wait impatiently for the moment when they will no longer be bound to the slightest show of effort. It is the greatest misery to realize that they spend all their days dishing out four or five years of jailtime, sending scores of men off to prison, and that every evening, when they return home, they don't feel like puking.

Even if they can't change the laws, even if the system is to blame, they should at least try to transform it or revolt. Aren't these judges Christian? Have they forgotten the catechism of their childhood? When man was banished from paradise he wasn't deprived of his spouse, he could still make a family, he wasn't completely destroyed—but these people destroy. They destroy so much more than the criminal whom they judge ever could.

From my seat of the accused, I rejected them. My silence denounced the farce of their questions. There they are, so busy skewing your "case," taking apart your life's mystery, debating whether your difficult childhood could be considered an extenuating circumstance—because obviously all evil stems from childhood. It's so insincere. They feign interest in you while having already forgotten and condemned you, because they don't expect to get to know you any better from your answers. They are merely confirming an already decided ruling.

"Clémenti's personality and behavior demonstrate both a physical and a psychological predisposition to the possession and use of drugs." This is what it comes down to: no one to blame but yourself. Your mouth and your ideas are testimony enough.

"But there's no proof!"

"What do you mean? Just look at him!"

It's irrefutable. The judges would be hard-pressed to disavow this kind of self-incrimination, especially since it keeps their hands clean. They only acknowledge the obvious: the fact that all long-haired men are suspects, and all suspects are guilty.

For the bourgeoisie that is distraught because its sons don't want to look like their fathers, for all who, perched upon a moral order, cannot imagine that the world's children would ever be able to dream of an ideal other than "work, family, homeland," drugs become the easy answer. What made you refuse to serve your rank in this rotten society? What made you see only disorder, violence, exploitation, and injustice, where most see comfort and progress? What made you denounce the army, asylums, and prisons? Drugs, of course. The notion that drugs are only a repercussion of society's evils, a secondary effect, is an idea that very few people understand, and I think that a lot of people have a vested interest in making sure that it doesn't spread too far. It is infinitely preferable that drugs appear to be a primary cause, so they can explain away every problem without raising too many questions, and society can slash a hard line between who is "normal" and who is an outsider.

"I would like to talk to you about the hell that is your prisons—"

"Talk to us instead about your hellish drug addiction."

"I would like—"

"Don't listen to him, he's out of his mind."

From this point of view, the Italian law is perfect. It registers no difference between drug use, possession, selling, or trafficking. Anything remotely related to drugs receives the same treatment. "Anyone caught without authorization buying, selling, distributing, exporting, importing, transporting, obtaining for others, using, or holding substances or preparations included on the list of drugs is sentenced to prison for three to eight years and is subject to a fine of 300,000 to 400,000 lire." Simply put, this means that the guy caught smoking a joint is fined the same amount as someone caught dealing two kilos of heroin. The addict is treated like the trafficker: prison, not rehab. The judges may still nuance the sanctions, but the law leaves little room for change.

At the very least, my trial triggered a series of polemics in Italian newspapers regarding the merits of this law. Lawyers and deputies called for its modification or abolition because to equate drug trafficking and drug use (even simple possession) contradicts the constitutional principle of equality before the law: the same sentences for the same cases, different sentences for different cases. The cases of the trafficker and the addict are surely distinct. The newest law, passed eight days after the end of my second trial, sends the trafficker to prison and the addict to rehab.

I hope that I contributed to this amendment. I hope, more than anything, that the one hundred and fifty men I met in prison—most of them locked up for just a pipe—will be released, and that their spots will never be filled. I told them that when the law is unjust, it's up to the judges to play a role in correcting it, no matter how small the deviation; to take responsibility instead of shrinking behind the text, sighing to themselves, *It is what it is, what else can we do?* It's up to the judges to grant a ruling more generous than what the system authorizes, more generous than the system itself. And, well, my judges didn't buy it! They couldn't just enforce the law in its idiotic austerity, so they felt obliged to justify it. The very text that condemned me congratulates the law for being itself: "The lawmaker proposes to unequivocally eradicate the pest of addiction with widespread, radical action and regulation. We unanimously recognize the need to suppress drug trafficking at the level of retail distribution, and this could never succeed if we didn't *also* punish those who feed this traffic for one reason or another, with or without lucrative purposes, because the vice is what brings about drug distribution and, ultimately, wholesale drug trade."

In other words, to eradicate the sickness, let's kill the sick. Addicts are the true instigators because they carry the defect within them; the traffickers are just businessmen.

When I heard this hypocritical, nauseatingly servile couplet, and realized that this was why they gave me two years, I knew that I had been right to meet them with silence, to let them go to the end of their logic. I felt immense joy, a confirmation that my place was right there, on the outcast's bench, in prisons, and that from then on I needed to use the time given to me to accomplish the most important task of my life: to fight and create with my imprisoned brothers. I returned to Regina Coeli and was proud of this conviction because my judges had ultimately condemned innocence, they had condemned creation, they had condemned life—they had condemned themselves. I accepted this period of time and together, with my brothers, we created.

Farewell to the Idol

There came a day when I felt the need to go beyond the words of the poem. These words had to come alive and become active gestures. And for me, this movement was made possible by life's poetry: theater and cinema.

A buoy at sea,
a hotel room inside an inkwell,
a bed with friends.

The soft voice of the street that groans with conquests,
with power struggles in the ghetto,
how many have committed suicide?

How many have you devoured?
Do you believe that the Principle of your principles
will go on?

I do not believe it. I know now what I did not know then.
I will follow the road until the lights go out,
and the monologue of existence,

*from asylum to connection,
to cinema, the art of survival.*

I love cinema because its images are traces of something forgotten, a lost part of you. Suddenly, in a flash, you are reacquainted with your past: I was once that man who runs across the screen. And at the very moment you're playing the part, you become the person who will one day look back at yourself. A film is like a bridge that connects you to others as much as it does to yourself, to who you were and who you weren't. It's a meeting place between brothers who don't know each other, whose fates are merged by happenstance across time and space.

* * *

After Jean-Pierre Kalfon, I met Marc'O. He was in his own world and I was in mine. One day, I heard that he was looking for someone to fill a role so I went to him. He was rehearsing a play with Bulle Ogier.

"So," he sighed, "we have this play that we'd really like to put on, but we don't have any money."

I asked him to let me read some of what he'd written, a play called *Spring*. It seemed so brilliant that I just went for it, I did the play. I invited the Saint-Germain crowd to the premiere—Jean-Pierre, Barbout, the whole gang. And that's how the troupe began, with this chance encounter with a great man and a wonderful actress.

We worked together for four or five years. We started some of the first *café-théâtres* in Paris. It was amazing for us, because we didn't have to wait years for the possibility of showing our work. We could do what everyone in theater dreams of: write a script, rehearse it, and perform it straightaway. To realize our ideas in real time, refine them, live them out. This taught us a lot, drawing continually from our lived experience of the stage, and being constantly confronted with the audience, the most active element in theatre. It prevented us from experimenting in a vacuum. Each time we tried to go a little further, but it always came from a shared experience: we never cut ourselves off from the audience because it was always in front of them, with them, that we bore out new ideas, and tested the limits of our explorations.

Marc'O's troupe was an ark and a journey. It was five years of collective work, excess, initiation and invention; a community of men and women uniting their strengths in order to come together around the same source, all of us fed by the same energy, giving everything to the group. And we never let professional or personal competition get in our way. This type of communal work and life taught me a lot, even though it eventually became difficult for the troupe to evolve, with the same people always working together. The quality of the work declined, and we were going in circles.

After *Les Bargasses*, we started getting some more recognition, which contributed to the success of *The Idols*. The film was a satire about the world of show-business, the yé-yé phenomenon, the ideology and mythology surrounding the radio show *Salut les copains*; but it was also a film about us, about that important moment in our lives: the foreshadowing of the troupe's disintegration. It is the fate of every troupe to eventually break up, to come to the end of the road. And we'd wanted to capture this moment when we were all forced to choose, and then follow, our own paths. The film was a public event not only because we talked to audience members and gave them a glass of red wine during the show, but because we were engaged and implicated in all of it. Theater was reconnected with life.

Tradition wants actors to be automatons that perform at the press of a button, machines made to make people laugh or cry on command. We wanted something else. We thought that playing a role meant partaking in an adventure that would shake up our own lives. This is why the troupe carried a great violence within it, and we knew that this violence would eventually destroy our group. But we also knew that this force could serve us in a positive way, so we used the stage to focus and reappropriate this violence. We wanted to make the audience share in our rage so they could leave this two-hour journey with renewed energy. I hope that our violence helped the audience see things a little more clearly, to make them understand how our lives were rigged by a system that boxed us into houses, factories, and prisons, all for "the good of the nation."

There was a choice that each of the troupe's stars had to confront: keep moving freely among the various opportunities in theater, cinema, and television—as we had done up until that point—or be reeled in by business and wheeler-dealers and "talent" scouts whose gimmicks were intended to buy your subservience with beautiful cars, beautiful apartments, and beautiful women. By using *The Idols* to condemn this system and criticize the machine that manufactures idols and hurls them into the market, we were simply performing our refusal to enter into its game and become commercial products, as well as our unwillingness to benefit from the privileges normally attached to money. These privileges are only ever entry tickets into a golden prison that you are locked inside, forced to do what investors want, never what *you* want.

There were men who spent their entire lives in pursuit of new faces, fresh meat. For example, they offered to break us into the music industry—all we had to do was sign contracts and slave away for a year, and then we would be superstars. We didn't fall for it. We were saved by our violence, our need for independence. By acting out the role of idols, we refused to become them, though the small crowds of the *café-théâtres* would occasionally see us that way. But this small fame had nothing to do with what the industry wanted to exploit, because the *café théâtres* weren't profitable for anyone. Above all, the idol is the little mafia's money-making machine. And as soon as the idol isn't making enough money, his publicity stops and he is left to die, like a statue fallen from its pedestal, smashed to pieces on the floor. He gave everything, and now nothing is left. The idol was used up to his last drops of creativity and capital; he became an empty shell. Useless, dead.

I hate being managed. I like staying open to any adventures fate has for me. My "career," as they say, will never be regulated, controlled, or planned years in advance by a brain trust. I think that freedom—even if it comes with difficulties, squalor, discomfort—is the only thing that allows you to create with your heart, so you can give the people a message that doesn't alienate them and which gives them strength to break out from the prisons that are systematically designed to exploit your soul. I know it's difficult—practically impossible in France's morally corrupt entertainment industry—to keep going, to stay true to yourself, to maintain the purity that gives meaning to all creation, all the while "fulfilling contractual obligations," satisfying the interests of the businessmen who bet on you. Either you sell yourself and thus empty yourself out, or you stay on the fringes and fight for your ideas.

* * *

Roman judges, this is why I found your insistence so appalling—your desire that I adhere perfectly to your idea of what a "movie star" is. For you, an actor both famous and broke does not exist. In order to make an example out of my trial and conviction, you needed me not only to be a known actor, but to have deep pockets. What's incredible is the fact that I had to find witnesses to prove that notwithstanding my career and the films I'd acted in before being jailed, I wasn't rich, and nowhere close to being able to afford to indulge in drugs.

"How is that so, considering you were acting in films back-to-back?"

"Your Honor, you ought to get to know the films I worked on."

"You were the star?"

"Yes, but to be the star—to use *your* word—of independent, low-budget films is to be paid even less than an extra in a blockbuster."

How could I get him to understand that you cannot make a living on the films made by young filmmakers? When you're picking the scripts, you're not shooting every day for the industry. When I really like someone, or really like a project, I work for nominal wages and often for free—those are my politics. But that wouldn't fit into your design. Clémenti is a star, stars are loaded, thus he is loaded. Stars do drugs, so he uses his money to pay for a fix. And so on. Have you even thought about it for a second? I doubt it. So much seems self-evident to those who subscribe to the myth of the star.

"Regarding the actor's alleged financial difficulties which would have prohibited him from procuring the drugs, the court observes that Pierre Clémenti had in fact earned considerable amounts of money. Before his arrest, he had received approximately twenty offers to be the lead of just as many films, and three days before being arrested, he had accepted an offer from French television to play in a TV movie. The facts at hand thus prove, on the basis of common sense, that Clémenti had at his disposal large and indubitable monetary resources, and that they were expected to become even greater in the immediate future. Therefore, it seems preposterous that the defense argues, based on the testimony of an employee at the William Morris Agency, that Clémenti is destitute, jobless, looking for work and money."

"Gentlemen, gentlemen, work and money do not necessarily go together."

And I hope you'll allow me to admire your appeal to "common sense"—indeed, what better than that to uphold your logic? The myth is total, urgent, and you fall victim to it, even if you haven't stopped fighting to break the image of the star.

The majority of the actors who "make it" are not immune. They reach Olympus, take their place among the demigods, and believe in the flaming myth that deifies them and which they stoke with each spectacle of their promoted life. Can't these idols—I hate the thing and the very word—provoke something other than clichéd desires and empty dreams? Lust for luxury, shows, vanity, and money brainwashes young minds more dangerously than drugs. There it is, the real opium. It misdirects one's energies from the creative path, dries hearts, and channels one's living forces towards the shabby, toxic goal of individual "success."

I think it's a lot more important for the actor to grow into himself authentically, to learn from the simplicity of daily life and communicate with his people, to let his work illuminate truth, and turn away from all that is fake, artificial, illusory. The actor is the representative of the collective unconscious; his work allows him to be conscious of his bliss or his sorrow, to perpetuate the former and bring the latter to an end, and to find the way towards happiness. The actor can spark a fire from which anyone may draw the warmth and energy to keep going.

I think that art must be for the people, which is why I don't think it can be reconciled with the idol who is placed above the people, who dominates and disgraces them, who is served by them. I see the artist as a worker among the rest. He must accomplish his daily task: to embody joy and suffering with sincerity and humility. He must also never stop looking, developing his experience and his knowledge, and more than anything he must never stop at the goals and tools offered to him by the system. To stop there is to die.

The Road

When I acted on a stage for the first time (I was a Templar) and realized that I had to think about a script, stage directions, and my voice and body in space, I became blocked, awkward, and tense. I had the eerie impression of having entered into a universe where everything, absolutely everything, was unknown; where foreign laws ruled everything down to the smallest phenomenon, the briefest act, and the most common things in the world—like saying "Hey!" or leaving the room—became strange to me. Jean-Pierre Kalfon laughed kindly at my panic and seemed not the least annoyed by this paralysis. I attributed this generosity to his experience.

"Don't worry! Listen, we are all beginners here, and I hope that we'll stay that way for a long time, because it's our strength. Just do what you can, and forget any models you may have in mind."

I would remember this whenever I approached a new role: I must always be a beginner who is open to all discoveries, and never let myself be locked into a style, a system of habits, or the old collection of ticks that is considered to be a sign of maturity in an actor. Real creativity is only possible when you do everything as if for the first time, when you refuse to be satisfied by long-honed technique and experience. Every time you begin, you must confront problems that reveal themselves to be so radically new that your experience cannot solve them—and this is a good thing. Your experience is a burden, an obstacle that you must break out of. You must be a virgin before the new.

It didn't take long for me to understand that the industry was uninterested in virginity. Its prime objective was not the facilitation of this search; it did not aim to disrupt habits or risk itself for the unprecedented. Far from it. The industry functions according to the principle of repetition, regurgitating successful formulas to the point of exhaustion. After *Benjamin*, producers only ever saw me as an innocent adolescent. And after *Belle de Jour*, as a dangerous bad boy. It's not enough to fight to create a new image of yourself: first you must reject the steady stream of projects that offer you (for a good deal of money) the opportunity to imitate yourself by dragging out your preceding roles. There are so few filmmakers who really build something new and have the balls to go for the unknown. I had the chance to meet some of them, and I didn't indulge the others.

* * *

The great encounter, the one that determined a lot of things for me, was with Buñuel. I'd been told, "You'll see, he's strange. You never know what he's thinking, you can't tell if he's joking or serious." I was told so many things: that he was a legend, he had the aura of a genius, he was particularly attuned to the mysterious and the strange. When I went to meet him, I was crippled with terror and wild with hope at the same time.

I was immediately struck by one thing: his face was the only thing you saw. His unbelievable features, worn down by life; his thick, pockmarked skin; his sunken eyes whose black shadow contained a vivid light. I couldn't say a word from where I was, I don't even remember if it was in a production office, an apartment, or a hotel room. All I know is that I was looking into the immeasurable shore of his face, the clear water of his gaze.

I'd been told, "Speak loudly, we don't know if he's deaf or if he's just pretending not to hear." But how to speak? I knew that this couldn't go on, I had to say something, I was sure that my silence, my insistent stare, must have been unnerving. Surely someone else would have addressed me, someone else would have started talking, if only to lessen the awkwardness. But it was enough for Buñuel to look at me like that, simply and straightforwardly, as if we had met only so we could look at one another, and words were unnecessary.

Eventually someone walked in, perhaps an assistant, I don't remember who. Buñuel turned towards him.

"This is Clémenti. Show him the script."

If I understood correctly, I'd just been hired for *Belle de Jour*.

* * *

Later I would see his hands, digger's hands, laid flat down on his thighs when he was sitting, like the farmers from the South who sit on their porch all day waiting for night to fall. He didn't give many suggestions on set, not to the technicians and not to the actors. If a problem arose—once it was impossible to film a traveling shot as he'd originally planned—it didn't matter to him. The other way would work just as well.

No filmmaker I've ever worked with has cared as little about aesthetic concerns than Buñuel. For anything related to a film's style, or even to the script—colors, frames, lights, movements—he deferred entirely to his team. A few rehearsals, even fewer edits, a vague idea of the setup, and then we were rolling. It was the simplest process in the world. This was possible because the film was already built, the characters and situations were so strong, the script was so solid, that we only had to follow our character's arc and realize their destiny just as Buñuel had clearly and ineluctably intended. It was as if the mere presence of the filmmaker, in all his passive glory, was enough to ensure that the puzzle would be put together.

I have never felt this degree of self-confidence from another director. No one else possesses Buñuel's rigorous vision of the end and the certainty of how to get there. Nothing—no on-set accidents, no acting difficulties—is more important than the quiet force of the idea that governs the entire film from its conception to its production; this idea is never weighed down by the details. Working with Buñuel teaches you the importance of economy and simplicity. You learn to hold onto only that which is necessary and strictly useful, in service of the one principal thing: the ruling logic of the dream. And, without Buñuel having to ask you, you let go of the embellishments and effects to which you're so often tempted to cling, and in which you ultimately lose yourself.

But this simplicity is subtle. The rogue in *Belle de Jour* isn't a clear-cut character. He is like all of Buñuel's characters: doubled, ambiguous, undecided; angelic and devilish, beautiful and ugly, violent and calm. In prison, I met men like him who were both pure and putrefied, serious, coursing with flashes of madness. The Christ-Devil in *The Milky Way* wasn't easy to crack, either. But the contradiction that strikes at the heart of all these characters is what constitutes their strength and their truth. Buñuel gives his actors neither explanations nor instructions regarding the psychology of their roles, because all of it goes beyond psychology. What could he possibly explain? Actions and behaviors lead to logical, albeit contradictory, consequences. As such, Buñuel didn't need to talk much, just like the father who knows the dreams of his children and helps to carry them out, regardless of their mistakes.

* * *

Sometimes you just couldn't handle it anymore and, over dinner, someone from the team would take the plunge, asking Buñuel about the meaning of the scene we'd just shot. He played deaf, but you could tell from his ironic smile that he'd heard the question.

They asked again. "But why?"

"I promise you, there's nothing to understand."

"But that can't be true, there must be some symbolic importance…"

That's how he got upset—or pretended to get upset—and cut you off. He would say, "I don't know any more about it than you do. You are looking for something I'm not looking for."

I imagine that if he were asked about the meaning of roads in his most recent films, *The Milky Way* or *The Discreet Charm of the Bourgeoisie*, he would answer, "To walk on." My answer is that roads let you travel, they allow you to wander endlessly in the heart of a country that echoes with familiarity but which you're unable to recognize. They get you closer to your own hidden truth.

The Illuminated Court

I was put back in handcuffs.

"This hearing will resume in two hours."

Italian handcuffs are astounding. First of all, they are much heavier than French handcuffs. And infinitely more barbaric. They have nothing in common with the steel bracelet that closes easily around each wrist, linking one to the other while maintaining some comfort. Italian handcuffs are more like an instrument of torture. The black metal bars, more than half a foot long, flank the wrist like a noose, and their notches allow the guards to forcefully adjust them and, at their whim, tighten them just a little bit more...

The rifleman was used to this mechanism. He left some space between the metal and my skin. He must have known that I was hardly in a state to resist. I'd been slouching into the bench all morning. I was distant and daydreaming and, whenever my attention would snap back to the hearing, depressed by the ridiculous clown show in progress. I was excited for the afternoon session because then I'd no longer be in the spotlight, alone in front of the three judges. It was now the witnesses' turn.

When I saw Fellini come into the room, entering through the side door to approach the stand, I felt as though they were judging him, too. Even the common witness, a stranger to the case who wanted to give a deposition in solidarity, must have felt the immense weight of justice bearing down upon them before the judges, the ceremonial apparatus of the magistrate. To experience this weight is to be in the position of the accused, the judgeable. You are there because you responded to the court's invitation to testify for a friend and play your hand in helping him leave, but as soon as you're at the stand you're no longer a part of the audience. You're on stage participating in the performance, the questions are now aimed at you, and they are trying as hard as they can to make you confess.

* * *

I had never worked with Fellini, but I'd met him when he was preparing Fellini Satyricon. He'd asked me to be in it. At that point my hair had grown past my shoulders. He approached me and smoothed back my hair, freeing my face.

"You should show your ears. You have the pointy ears of a wolf, you shouldn't hide them."

He told me that for him, film was, above all else, a succession of heads, a parade of faces. "I spend months looking at faces, ten hours per day. I put advertisements in Rome's popular newspapers: Fellini is looking for bakers, maids, fishermen. They come by the hundreds. They go through my office, one or two minutes, max. I sift through the faces. The Roman people have the most marvelous faces in the world. Among them, you find traits of the old race, mixed, transformed, changed by time, burdened or deformed to the point of caricature. I take their pictures, and for hours afterwards I compare them, I pair them, I construct scenes between isolated faces. Once I've finished, once I've chosen my gallery of portraits, it's as if the film is already made. Everything that follows—the set, costumes, dialogue, even the narrative—is the direct consequence of these everyday men and women whose faces I have fallen in love with."

I'd also fallen in love with Fellini and his head, which resembled the heads in his films, but at that moment in my life, I didn't really want to work with him because his sets looked like factories, especially for Fellini Satyricon. It was like the Fiat factory, with hundreds of actors, thousands of workers, extras, and artisans at work for months, an entire city to build and populate, basically an army. I told him that I didn't want to be the umpteenth person to get into that mess, it didn't really make a difference whether a painter or bricklayer with pointed ears took my place. He knew that if I accepted, it would only be to get some money from the producers. I told him that we should wait for a smaller project if we wanted to do something different together. I think he was a bit unhappy with me for this reason, and yet there he was, at the witness stand, his hair as unruly as ever.

* * *

"What do you have to say in defense of the accused?"
"Your Honor…"

* * *

I have a lot of love for Italian filmmakers—Fellini, Visconti, Pasolini, Bertolucci, De Sica, Brocani. I think they are the direct heirs of the Renaissance spirit. They have a sense for beauty and finesse, but they are not cut off from the people. They don't operate as an elite and they're not some aristocracy of artists who profit from the system like parasites—and yet they have "arrived," so to speak. I think they really work for the working class, the Italian multitudes, and with their vast, longstanding culture, they serve life itself.

For example, Pasolini is, in his own way, like Saint Paul because he wants to be the harbinger of the nation's spirit. He thinks he has a mission to liberate the Italian people from the moral norms and Catholic rules that have castrated them for centuries, and which have made them shameful of their sexuality. He probed the working-class roots of Italian culture and found a great moral freedom therein. Through his films, he told people, "This is who you were. Why did you change? What do you all want? To have women, make love?" Pasolini painted great erotic frescoes and captured the figures of the most beautiful women in the world. It was as if he was sending slightly pornographic postcards to thousands of his friends.

Italy is changing, sexual taboos are collapsing, there are fewer complexes—and yet the report of my arrest detailed that Anna-Maria's apartment had been surveilled for several months because the neighbors complained about the "orgies" that were held there. We had run into naked girls on the landing. We heard cries of passion every night. There were parties that lasted until dawn. What a scandal. You see, Pasolini, you still have some work to do!

* * *

The presiding judge seemed to be in awe of that fact that Fellini was talking to him. And I think the other judges were impressed, but they didn't want to show it; they had an affected arrogance, as if their robes detached them from the realm of all human emotion.

"I met with Clémenti twice. The first time, I spent several days with him. I had chosen him for one of the roles in Fellini Satyricon, I spoke to him for a long time, and I never had the impression that he was on drugs. He seemed to me to be an endearing person who inspires sympathy and tenderness, who seeks advice and who's concerned about understanding all of the nuances of his work. In sum, he is a conscientious actor and an exquisite person."

* * *

You said all this calmly, your voice was steady, and I was at once proud and ashamed, because all the Italian artists came with you to testify that I was ultimately one of them. I had done more work in Italy than in France, on films that were more important, or at least more meaningful to me. The presence of Fellini and De Sica at the trial made it seem as though all Italian artists were there in solidarity, opening themselves up to the risk of two years in prison. It was a collective protest against a trial that was itself a form of censorship.

Italian cinema has never shied away from criticizing injustice, scandal, and the wrongdoings of the police and the criminal justice system. So, every once in a while, power tightens its grip because it understands the undeniable force of artists, intellectuals, and journalists in Italy, and it dreads their strength. These were the artists who fought for Valpreda, who relentlessly worked to expose the lies and investigate the police's biases. These were the artists who criticized the penal code, the system of preventive detention, and the courts' calculated slowness.

It's thanks to them that the police don't lock up more people, don't kill more, don't fake more suicides of men who get in their way. I think it requires a lot of courage to lead such a fight, because the policing powers are so strong that no one in Italy, not even the famous artists, can escape their threats. There have been trials against Pasolini, Bertolucci, and so many others. All it takes is some anonymous letter, a made-up story about a girl or a boy, or a bogus search where cops "find" some drugs at your place. Telephone conversations are constantly tapped and your meetings are spied on; everyone is inevitably at the mercy of the police because they can send you to jail if they deem your arrest necessary to maintain their established order, even if your name is Fellini.

That's why your solidarity moved me and restored my confidence. Light entered the courtroom and illuminated the judges' souls. They were probably going to condemn me anyway, but that was less important now that they wouldn't be condemning me alone.

The meaning of my presence on that bench in a Roman court was becoming increasingly clear. First and foremost, the witnesses were telling me, "Pierre, don't worry. You weren't wrong to choose Italy as the country of your heart. You weren't wrong to like working with us, for us. We have come to testify that you have found your brothers here."

* * *

Nearly ten years have passed since I walked out of the Stazione Termini in Rome, the country's vibrant center through which all paths cross and converge. And during those ten years, I think I spent more time in Italy than in France. I love this country and its people, even if I have no sympathy for its ruling class who are hopelessly rotten and enslaved to profit, who treat the poor like slaves valued only for their sweat. But the nation is great and strong, despite its deep-seated divisions between North and South, between one region and another, between cities and the countryside, despite having suffered the Church's age-old oppression, despite having weathered fascism's long purge. I feel good here, and I bask in this kingdom of families and children, this fermented, fertile land.

* * *

When I was hanging around Saint-Germain, I ended up getting to know all the local celebrities. Alain Delon was getting a lot of acting jobs at that point, and he knew I was completely broke, adrift. One evening, I met him just around the corner from Café de Flore. "Come," he told me, "I will bring you to Rome. I'm shooting a film for Visconti and I'm sure he'll find you something, at least a small role." Of course I went. I left just like that, in jeans and a leather jacket. There was a citywide celebration the next day.

I met Visconti in the courtyard of his palace. He walked towards me, laughing, and took my hands in his. "For a greaser, you have the hands of a prince."

That's how I ended up in The Leopard, and more importantly how I started to fall in love with Italy.

The Evening Mail

Naturally, we appealed.

Dear Pierre,
Don't give up. And don't forget that as long as the final verdict has yet to be decided, you are not convicted. You are still in preventive detention, even if we know that this changes practically nothing for you.
Your lawyer, Paolo Appella

This is what happens: you feed off of hope, promises, and attention from the law, and this enables you to endure the severity of the facts at hand. I was beaming in the courtroom when the ruling was decided, but this joy in being right, just like a martyr's elation, didn't last long. I felt nauseous when I returned to my cell in Regina Coeli. I started painting furiously, and with a savage passion I smeared green paint upon the image of my judges. This way, they too would be damned by their image, just as they'd damned me for my own: "It is indisputable that Clémenti's physical appearance embodies the characteristics of a drug addict." My judges, you are all beautiful. Your appearance speaks volumes, too. One need not look at you for long to see that you're full of shit.

Dear Pierre,
Don't worry, we are making progress. We asked that the appeal be expedited. We stressed that if the decision takes too long, your acquittal would go into effect only after you'd have already spent two years in preventive detention, essentially serving the sentence for a crime you won't even be convicted of.
Your lawyers, F. Ungaro and P. Appella

When the evening mail comes, you need strength to read the letters that are written to comfort you, but which nonetheless throw a harsh light on the absurdity of your situation. Even more than the cell, you're imprisoned within a peculiar logic, a Kafkian mechanics.

Italian law stipulates a maximum of two years for preventive detention. It also dictates, for charges of drug possession, a minimum sentence of two years. Yet the law doesn't allow the right to interim release for those accused of drug possession. And because justice is unwise and slow, your time in preventive detention is often more than two-thirds served before the court deems you guilty or not, well before your actual sentence begins (that is, if you're not acquitted).

According to this logic, the stakes are pretty low: innocent or guilty, you'll be in prison for at least one year. That's what you get for looking suspicious. It is within these contradictions that the true nature of bourgeois law begins to reveal itself. In principle, and in terms of "democracy," the law preaches that every suspect will be presumed innocent until proven guilty. But the court's daily practice reveals an altogether different story: they'd rather jail you than hurry up, and lock up innocents as long as they aren't proven to be innocent—at least long enough to wear them down.

You're still talking about innocence? What innocence? The innocence of a prisoner or convict doesn't carry the same weight as that of someone who is really free! Even if better judges decide to acquit you, they are unable to return the wasted months of your life, and they can't erase this simple fact: you went to prison. And you can bet that there'll be, at one point or another, a policeman, a court of law, or even a well-meaning person who believes, after all, that "no one goes to jail for no reason," that there's no smoke without fire. Going to prison is like losing your virginity—afterwards, you're forever changed. And sure, you made it out, and there will come a time when you'll forget having ever been there, but your record remains, and the memories, too. Because despite all you did to erase it from your mind, the prison is inscribed within you.

This is how you come to understand how fragile the notions of innocence and guilt really are. The official task of State institutions (courts, police forces, prisons) is to distinguish between the innocent and the guilty, yet because they fail to acknowledge the fragility of these definitions—either for personal incompetence or outright politics—you realize that the problem isn't about "blunders," "errors," "unfortunate circumstances," or "rare exceptions," even though that's the only story being reported and repeated by the press, which serves only the powerful. You realize that this violence is indeed the rule, the underlying logic of the entire system.

In a society built on repression, who is innocent? Who isn't guilty? Wherever you go, you hear only one refrain: lock them all up! First and foremost, lock them up—in asylums, barracks, prisons, schools. Lock them up, and only afterwards will their cases be considered, only then will each be allowed to claim his rights and be judged. This is a society of scares and slaps: hit first, talk later. Anyone who falls outside the "norm" (be it for their hair, ideas, or morals) is quickly beaten back into it, and if that doesn't work, they are just as soon locked up, handcuffed, straightjacketed, tossed behind bars and barbed wire.

Prison can be an excellent political school, but only if you try to pierce the mystery of what is happening to you. Before I went to prison, I thought of politics as a realm of abstraction, a science reserved to specialists or an elite group of intellectuals. But in prison I learned that politics were singularly responsible for why and how the world functions, and why we occupy this place of suffering. I also learned that politics could be an instrument of happiness.

The struggle inside prisons thus takes on new meaning. It's not only about improving the prison conditions that determine the daily fate for thousands of detainees, nor about alleviating the harshness that is painstakingly and conscientiously inflicted upon prisoners every day—and those are already hefty goals! It's not enough to strip them of their freedom, their bodies and minds must also be punished! It's important to open up the prison's gates so everyone can see that prison is society's logical end. Prisons are a loyal portrait of the regimes that create and manage them. They reveal their hypocrisy. On the basis of their prisons, we can judge the defenders of "individual freedom"— the "liberals," "democrats," and all who have the audacity to consider themselves missionaries of the "free world." Their idea of freedom is only worth as much as their prisons. Oppressive, unjust, and rotten, just like them.

The prisoner desires nothing so much as liberty, but the practice of prison ends up teaching him that he has been lied to about the advantages of this freedom: he will not be free as long as others are still in prison, and he will not be a man as long as others are treated like dogs. I hope, my brother, that you eventually understand that a society that authorizes these kinds of prisons must be transformed as quickly as possible. New blood must drown the old cells.

* * *

The evening mail also brought me news of the trial. Polemics abounded in the Italian press. These articles shed light on the absurdities of the drug laws, which happened to contradict other articles of law. These articles also emphasized the incoherence of a legislation that prohibited interim release for someone who was picked up smoking a joint, whereas the "ordinary" criminal who scammed his neighbors or his boss could wait calmly in his home until the judge had the time to reach a decision. These articles questioned whether the first example was really more "dangerous for society" than the second. They also pointed out that despite its democratic and Christian rulers, Italy had not yet ratified the United Nations Convention on the repression of the drug business, which stipulates that drug addicts be put in the care of doctors, not prison guards.

Dear Pierre,
We are forwarding you an important statement that was made by psychiatrist Sebastiano Fiume:
"In conclusion, a part of society diagnoses the illness, or, better yet, the sickness, after which it entrusts its [...] therapeutic treatment to the other part of society which relies on the penal system for a cure. In the final analysis, the acknowledgment de jure of the sickness is contradicted de facto by a series of repressive interventions that disavow this acknowledgment: a sickness implies a cure, and should be free from all forms of repression, which is itself an insult to science and which, obviously, rarely heals anything."
You see that things are moving forward. Opinions are changing, no doubt thanks to your trial.
Don't lose hope.
Your lawyers.

This hardly comes as consolation when you're in the hole, but it's consoling nonetheless. I felt that now that I was back in prison, I could be helpful to those on the inside and on the outside. This is what kept me going, as well as letters, the news, French and Italian articles that were passed around during evening walks so as to avoid censorship. A network of solidarity began on the outside, in parallel to what already existed on the inside. This changes the prisoner's life and strengthens his capacity for resistance, since he can rely on the clandestine support of those who are free. Prisons are ultimately porous to the fraternity of men.

I fought really hard during my last weeks at Regina Coeli. I knew what to say to connect with my fellow prisoners. We were all riled up and once again, word of a prison-wide hunger strike began to spread. I think that's why the administration finally complied with my lawyers' prior request to get me transferred to Rebibbia, the supposedly less severe prison. I was making too much noise, I had too many allies. I would be quieter elsewhere.

It was still good news.

Dear Mother,
Don't lose your mind over my trial. God willing, the doors will open for me soon. Anyway, now I have enough strength to confront reality. Injustice has set me aflame. I hope my next home will be freer than this one. There isn't much happiness where I am, but experience has always been the best school of all...

A Single Spark Can Set
All Prisons Aflame

Before anything else, you notice the light. The glare of cells finally equipped with real windows, so bright that for the first few days you can't help but squint, your eyes having gotten used to Regina Coeli's dark holes. And, as if to refract and amplify this brightness, Rebibbia's cells are painted white. The contrast is brutal. You think to yourself, this is it, you can finally touch the harbor after sailing through the night. You realize that the golden legend that stirred the dreams of Regina Coeli's living dead is actually grounded in fact: they do exist, those more humane prisons that are so often held up as perfect examples. And from the outset, upon first sight, you are overcome by a sort of enthusiasm. Here, time is not totally lost, and inmates' energies are no longer fully exhausted from having to resist moral and material oppression every second. Here, there are still living forces that create.

Your first impressions of the "model prisoner" reinforce this hope. The rules really are much looser. The time allotted for walks is doubled—four hours instead of two for exercise and fresh air each day. Not only do you have the right to decorate the walls of your "room" to your taste—with more than just angry graffiti—but you can also invite friends over, pour them a cup of coffee.

The library's collection is not altogether paltry, nor is it obstinately opposed to material that could awaken the mind. At Rebibbia, I read a lot of poets who became my most precious friends in prison—Flaubert, Aragon. But I also read books by politicians like de Gaulle, of course, likely a gift from the French consulate, and authors one would not necessarily expect to find in a prison, such as Lenin or an anthology of Mao's writings.

The guards are also different, you can talk to them more easily than you could at Regina Coeli, and they seem less trapped and somehow more useful because they are left alone with prisoners less often. Rebibbia is the kingdom of "penitentiary advisors," psychologists, psychiatrists, doctors: an army of men paid by the State to follow your "case." You tell yourself, great, this is the dream, someone's taking care of me, now I'm more than just dead weight, and they aren't leaving me to drown, they are preparing for my release.

And TV, too. Two hours every evening, in a group. First, like everything else, you hail this innovation as a small revolution. You think of TV as the best way to maintain contact with the outside world. At least I'll know, once I'm released, what the world has gone through during my hibernation—what achievements have been made, which wars have been fought. I'm in lockstep with free men, even if my steps move in circles around a supervised courtyard.

You tell yourself a lot of things. But in a few weeks' time, the facts will dampen your delusions. The repression at Rebibbia is less visible, less immediately tangible, less raw than at Regina Coeli. But it's no less real. It's telling that the most grueling revolts have happened in this paradise.

"But what do the prisoners want? Aren't they happy here? We have given them everything."

"They will never be happy."

Sure, the oppression is less savage. But that makes it more rational, its mechanism more subtle, more scientific—thus more inexorable. Soon you understand that each of the advantages from which the prisoner supposedly benefits ends up turning against him. More freedom in prisons, more comfort, and less everyday dread end up changing the needs of imprisoned men. They become less elemental, less frustrated, and the question of what to do with one's spirit looms heavier now that the body is less endangered. It's all well and good to allow prisoners a more flexible and stimulating schedule and to prioritize socializing and recreation. But soon this relaxation gives way to the question, "What do we do with this time, this extra freedom?" Every step forward reveals the need to go even further and transform prison life even more.

The model prison is the kingdom of half measures. They improve hell, convert the institution, but they don't change its function; they don't go so far as to question its social purpose which, for the men locked inside, remains the only question of importance. They eliminate atrocities found in traditional prisons through obvious reforms—but it is scandalous that these reforms aren't more widespread. They return a shadow of human dignity to prisoners. Prisoners are not treated like cattle. Sure. Fine. But what plan do they have for the prisoners, now that they have been given the chance to think of themselves as more than just dying men? They make nothing available for prisoners to kill time with, because in the end, prison boils down to only that: the killing of time, of hours, days, months, years. It doesn't occur to them that this time could be used for something other than its own burial. You give them back a taste for life and free their energies instead of systematically taking them away, but you don't know what to do with them. You choose not to do anything and let them drift, every man for himself, or you exhaust yourselves by "channeling" their energies lest they rise up and splash you. You're afraid of getting dirty.

This is why the reformist directors of Rebibbia were stuck in a vicious cycle.

"They will never be happy. But they have books, a daily shower, television."

Let's talk about TV. Far from being some indispensable window into the world, it was the prisoner's drug. First of all, many programs were censored. Under the pretext that it had to please everyone because we all watched it together, any shows that were slightly cultural or inherently political were eliminated. What leftover scraps were thrown before thousands of fascinated eyes every night of the year? Sports—of course—as well as variety shows, the occasional film, and commercials.

Prisoners were no less stultified than the thousands of their "free" fellow citizens. And this television in a monastery, this constant teasing of luxury, frantic consumption, and romance—did they really believe that all those things would settle us down? (Marlene, how many prisoners have dreamt of your elusive body? We once watched four of your films in a row.) They taunted us with impossible pleasures, which naturally made us crazy with rage. So revolts rose against the slowness of the court system; the wardens no longer understood, and the experts were at a loss.

That's how it was with the TV. It should do more than give guys a hard-on for hours at a time, lighting them up with fantasy. They've had enough! TV should make them understand the problems ravaging the country while they're in prison. The television should serve as a means of return to society that isn't just provisional, not just some brief intermission between two sentences. Everyone needs educational television, but no one more than prisoners, who turn back into children in a world that has grown up without them.

But these are just my fantasies. I doubt that one day there will be a prison or society that makes them come true. It's not in the system's interests for prisoners to leave prison stronger, more knowledgeable, and more informed than they were when they entered.

Beyond the psychologists who contented themselves with "understanding us" without trying to explain anything, the priests and chaplains were the only people who wanted more than superficial change. This shows the strength of the Church in Italy—that the administration kept out of it. The priests were upfront with their goal: to help prisons become a place of reflection, development, and learning. At Rebibbia, we could see them every day, one to one. They bridged the gap perfectly between the prison and the outside world, but they went even beyond their roles as benevolent communicators and recruiters for mass. Each Saturday, they held a "luncheon," a small conference during which one of the priests came to read a passage from the Gospels. The meetings wouldn't last very long. Once, upon the first mention of Christ, someone yelled, "But Christ is here, in prison!" The speaker stopped and looked at us.

"It's true that Christ is here."

The discussion took off from there, not towards the subject of Christ but of prison.

We had to fight to be allowed to have other conferences, and not only religious ones. We harassed the wardens and tried to convince the resident psychologist, but it wasn't easy.

"Why do you want to observe us, what's the point? We're sick of you taking us for idiots. We want to learn."

They didn't really know what to make of it. They didn't know how to measure or quantify our demands, how to put them into statistics—what could all that mean? They weren't necessarily against the idea, by the way, but they had no clue where to begin.

"Just make a positive report, we'll deal with the rest."

"No! I can't do that. We are responsible for the programs here…"

"But there are no programs!"

We ended up getting a weekly course about drugs, because the Minister of Health had sent a doctor to examine Rebibbia's junkies. He was surprised, because until that point he had seen us one at a time, and he had questioned and examined us as if we were strange, diseased cases, and afterwards he would work on his book. But now, as a group, we could ask him questions. And he had to respond with a language that went beyond his medical lexicon. Eventually, over the course of a few group discussions,

I think he learned more from us than we learned from him. I think that these meetings and conversations that took place outside of the constraints of his questionnaire helped him evolve, and changed his conception of addicts as well as prisoners.

I imagine that at that point, he better understood these men who resembled Christ and his apostles, and realized that it was a criminal gesture to lock them up. They were brighter and healthier than so many others because they did no harm to anyone, and instead of sucking on the patriotic bottle they were fed by life itself—people, music, creation. It was better for them to embark on a one- or two-year journey with their brothers instead of serving in the military and marching for the State.

That lasted three weeks, and then the administration swooped down on the doctor. They said his behavior was scandalous and irresponsible. They forbid him from seeing us again. The prison administration is afraid of everyone, doctors and prisoners alike. The administration thinks that a prison doctor must stay in his office and wait for the line of consultations. It's out of the question for him to roam the hallways or have drinks with the prisoners. He was utterly castrated by the administration. But then they looked to him for explanations when there was a series of suicides among the prisoners.

"You haven't noticed anything unusual? But that's your job!"

Thus we entered into the cycle of revolts. We educated ourselves in the field. We learned something that can't be learned, neither at the Sorbonne, nor at Saint-Cyr, nor at Polytechnique, something worth more than all that is taught in those prestigious places: we learned to fight to get respect. To be united, to move together, to remain in solidarity despite any provocations or divisive maneuvers by the upper administration. Prisoners will always remember the extraordinary strength that comes from their unity. The administration remembers it, too. After each storm, they scatter men across the country's prisons. Everything must begin again and this takes time, but eventually flames will rise, and the doors will give.

Refusing Obedience

After fire come the ashes.

The revolts were subdued, and their organizers were scattered across other prisons. But they weren't the only ones to leave Rebibbia: the prison brought in a new warden. The administration, which had previously encouraged and protected the previous warden's savage methods of repression, was now obliged to "re-establish peace" by sending him on leave. Or rather on reserve, in case the brute was needed again. He kept his salary, of course, and was allowed to carry a gun: he had perpetrated such horrors that some prisoners' brothers, cousins, or friends would surely take care of him if they ever sniffed him out.

They also wanted to have me transferred. I was thought to be a troublemaker, a dangerous element. My lawyers held their ground, and I was allowed to stay. But I was going to be watched closely because they wanted to drain the life out of me. In any case, the atmosphere was totally changed, and the new prisoners were so happy to be in a more comfortable prison that it took them a long time to really get it. And then the administration made some promises, and the Parliament became involved. It was time for me to fall into a deep sleep.

Of these last months at Rebibbia before my appeal, I have only muddled and fragmented memories: flashes, islands of consciousness, letters I wrote, and pieces of what my friends were telling Roman journalists at the time. I think it was at this point that I began to drift away. You can't tell when madness takes hold of you—you don't know exactly when it starts to get under your skin. You don't know you're breathing it through your very pores and that it's being diffused into your blood—because with madness comes forgetting, which leaves no trace of itself behind. From the outside, I must have looked like a hibernating animal. Sleep and meditation. Healing stillness, blazing silence. I no longer left my lair, and renounced nearly all walks, visits, and conversations. Prostate, the doctors said. "But you don't understand that he is on the brink of insanity!" the lawyers cried out. I didn't want to see anyone at all.

My name is peace, and joy rises up in me.
When, through total control of one's breath, heaven's door opens and closes at your will, you can be like the mother bird, the spiritual embryo, and you can drown the power of the soul in purity and silence, match your intelligence to the brightness of the sun, shape your actions to the symmetry of the seasons, beat to the rhythm of regained life, radiate a light that reverberates out to all four corners of the earth...

I wrote, but it didn't feel like writing. It felt like screaming. Like my voice was being channeled through my hand. And how could I actually have written, since I don't remember having seen anything but darkness? I would tell myself, You are a monk of the Middle Ages, and with your staff and shell you shall embark upon the great mystic voyage. You are walking along the Milky Way.

I drew a Christmas tree and, along with a long letter, sent it to the Pope to wish him a Merry Christmas on behalf of all the prisoners locked within the Eternal City. I am a pilgrim of Saint James, and I am telling you, Pope, that the real place for the

Church is in the prisons. And its role on this earth is not to care for the salvation of souls, but the salvation of prisoners.

I made ten copies of this letter, and I made sure it was forwarded to newspapers, the president, embassies. But it wasn't published—they must have kept it in their archives. It was a beautiful manifesto. I asked the question: If Christ were to come back to this Earth, would you first give him back his House? And in what condition would you return it? I made a case for everything that the Church could be doing in prisons, which it wasn't doing at all. I suggested some immediate actions. First of all, in Rebibbia, there was a theatre with two thousand seats. Closed. And a fully functional cinema. Also closed. Even a big, brand-new church. They preferred the little chapel; even though all Italians are Catholic, only thirty out of Rebibbia's 700 inmates regularly went to mass. But why not open these cultural spaces right now? Why wait fifty years?

You before whom all doors open: open the doors! You like to do what is good, you prefer good over evil, you have the power, therefore if you don't do it, it is because you're already dead. Come back to life!

I thought the repressive machine would eventually get me by crushing each and every one of my resistances. The sweet highs and mystical longings I experienced were evidence of my defeat. It's not as if I was waiting in a deadly calm for winter to pass and the sun to rise again to warm my bones. When all possibilities of action seem blocked, meditation remains. But isn't that one of the system's surest tricks? They tie you up and lock you in, twice over—in prison, of course, but also in your dreams.

Dear Pierre,
We insist—you must talk to us. Your appeal is scheduled for December 6, and this is big news, but how do you expect us to prepare for it if you refuse our visits? Do you realize it has been nearly three months since you have seen anyone, even us?

We are very worried.
Your lawyers.

You must know when it's necessary to go too far. So far that the system cannot handle your journey and consequent absence. If you merely withdraw into yourself, stay in your lane, and refuse to comply with the habits that dictate and trivialize prison life, it's tantamount to giving up without a fight. The administration, prison guards, and medical professionals seem not the least disturbed by a "less involved" prisoner who is defeated, haunted by his dreams, and checked out most of the time.

This is the trap I was talking about: you can dream, but that won't stop the machine from working. It would rather you dream than be contentious, aggressive, or combative. But this changes entirely once your inner illumination pushes you beyond your limits and commits you to a more radical refusal. Your absences become a force of extreme negation. And your body starts bearing the scars of crisis. You will be the (still) living proof of the machine's very logic, and thus unacceptable to it. The machine destroys men, and if you look at me, you'll see that I'm the very portrait of destruction. The machine ravages bodies and breaks spirits. And I bring its truth to the most severe consequences. I am the most logical of its products.

I refused all food other than water and the daily bread and my cell became a dungeon, though it remained full of light. I refused to leave, stopped reading and watching TV, gave up chit-chat and all other daily distractions. In three months, I lost fifteen pounds. But it wasn't enough.

I did end up seeing my lawyers. It didn't reassure them in the least. As soon as the trial date was announced, they sent me a letter, strongly advising me to get a haircut so as not to scare the judges. Thus ending my isolation, I had my first official visit to the prison barber, an old prisoner who was quite skillful after ten years of practice. He couldn't believe it.

"You really want me to cut it?

He took my long, curly strands in his hands and pulled them out to fully appreciate their length.

"You're going to feel lighter."

His initial excitement—the joy of getting to work with such a thick head of hair, left untouched for five or six years—didn't last.

"Marco, listen up. Shave it all off."

"What?"

"You heard me."

"You're out of your mind!"

"All of it, Marco."

He went silent, but I knew he was sad and that after all he would have preferred to cut nothing than shave everything, despite his aversion to hippies. He set down the comb and scissors, and his shears tore trenches into the black mass of my hair. There is always a feeling of gravity attached to the act of giving up one's hair. He fell silent. And even though there were no mirrors in the barber's cell, I kept my eyes shut. I focused all my energy on the grating, hushed scraping of the clippers. I would tell myself, Father's hands are purifying you. They are performing upon you the ancient gesture that initiates all of Buddha's followers. They are breaking the threads that connect you to your past, they are cutting all your earthly attachments. By fasting and now going through this rite, you have escaped—no prison could ever contain you.

Seated in the Dark

"So, Monsieur Clémenti, they are telling me that you've been having some problems?"

The new warden had heard about everything: I'd shaved my head, I wasn't eating, I was spending hours seated in the lotus position, breathing deeply in and out, my eyes fixed faraway. My nonviolent protest had begun to offend him. He summoned me to his office.

* * *

Some days earlier, I had written a letter to Philippe Garrel: I am leading a monk's life without the mass. The Holy Spirit visits me often and helps me accept human injustice as the cross we all must bear. Within these walls, truth's total vision cannot lie. Who will believe what I know, which is that the most beautiful human experiences are found in solitude? I yearn for work, adventure, love. I yearn for you, for friends. I yearn for sincerity and truth—and it is within this yearning that I love you.

I was thinking, while writing this letter, that there was really something prophetic about cinema. The last two films that I shot in France—with Philippe, funnily enough: The Virgin's Bed and The Inner Scar—had foreshadowed what was happening to me in prison. Both featured a quest for refusal and peace. We had wanted to show how solitude, through asceticism and mysticism, can bend towards death-as-liberation, but also how this same solitude can open itself up to salvation—to the fraternity of creative spirits, a unity of action and progress. We wanted to show that the initiated man, who has liberated himself with solitude and rites, can rediscover the meaning of life, along with the peace that gives birth to the universal spirit. Our hypothesis was that if Christ came back now to this earth, he wouldn't be able to do much more because of the thousands and thousands of Christ figures in the West who are working to stop this earth from turning into hell.

* * *

"You know that your lawyers are telling journalists that you're going crazy?"

I don't answer.

"It's not true, of course…"

Silence.

"But what do you want? For me to be held responsible?"

You stay quiet, you let him talk. The less your refusal is understood, the more power it has.

* * *

It was a time of many letters. I wrote them almost every night, but I never sent them. I addressed them to friends around the world, but it was as if writing them was more important than whether or not they were read. These letters were a way of speaking to myself, rather than speaking to others about me. Reader, here is one I've never forgotten:

Françoise,

My body, my soul, and my spirit are happy, because I know that you are on the right path. I crossed the desert of suffering, and on this day when harmony can reach you, free of hypocrisy, I write to you, because you are still the one who knocked on my door and heard my voice. Tonight I am writing to you, but it is mostly just to send you this marvelous light that can heal all those whom the system vows to destroy. You are a young, innocent girl, and I want you to know that sometimes you must say nothing in order to avoid mechanization, that evil trap set by those who have chosen to defend property at all costs.

I remain, despite everything, barbarous and savage—I didn't receive the same affection as many other children. I belong to nature, for it replaced the father I never knew. I believe that once more I will spend Christmas among the poorest souls—like me, they still aspire to happiness. Here I have seen people who are truly pure, for they have preserved the original language that allows people of all stripes to love each other, here in this prison in which they've been locked up by justice. On my own, I have always looked for the meaning of this wonderful journey that all men embark upon from birth.

It is difficult for man to rediscover a natural life. For those who carry the stigma of this policing society, it's hard to find new ground, a new world without terror in which one can live freely among his brothers and sisters, beyond violence, and without the threat of relapse. Upon their liberation, an invisible chain connects prisoners to a system that refuses to forget, a system determined to hold back those who have already given their entire lives to pay the debts of their youth.

I completely stopped working, because you must not be afraid of stopping everything in order to better understand what's in front of you. I quit creating, because energy comes from the sun and here, seated in the darkness assigned to me, my entire body suffers. I can't read anymore—the words have become a mirror in which I lose myself. Night comes, the small cells around mine are half-open for the daily spectacle of the third televised eye, a kind *of brainwashing that serves those in power: it makes the viewers docile, and makes them believe that everything is okay. I stopped going to these viewings. I could no longer watch a program until its end, and my eyes would just close shut.*

Now I am ageless because my spirit forgets all pleasures. And was I ever made happy by anything other than illuminations? I went to rock bottom so as not to be aimless anymore. This is also why I no longer write every night, as I did before: to avoid the contagion of routine that kills all sense of spontaneity. I shaved my head. Why? I don't know, perhaps as a way of asking God to liberate prisons, to put an end to the State's injustices. Perhaps I obeyed a desire to be pure? Perhaps it's a symbolic act for my brothers so they stop dying in these Italian concentration camps. In any case, with or without hair, prison remains the same, and I'm not sorry to be living like a newborn, aspiring to an innocence that awakens me from the daily asphyxiation.

Françoise, I'd like to talk to you about Balthazar. I love him. Yes, I love that wonderful child. Love and nature gave him to me. I'm afraid of not being good enough, yet I have the immense desire to be near him, to learn from him once again...

* * *

It was also around this time that my agents tried to bring me back to life and light, teasing me with film projects and promises of future roles. Acquitted or not, I would leave within six months. They made sure that I knew that offers were not scarce. I'm afraid to have disappointed them with my response: "I'm done with pseudo-intellectual films. I want to save my strengths for films devoted to all the world's children, and through very simple parables I want to make them discover life's mysteries; to teach them that the unremitting fight of good against evil will one day restore peace on earth. I no longer want to compromise myself in a dishonest industry that wastes the cultural possibilities of cinema for profits, and which produces nothing but human foolishness."

* * *

"Be serious, Monsieur Clémenti! Your lawyers have contacted your wife. She has come with your son. They are here now. You're not going to refuse to see them, are you?"

Balthazar and Margareth had heard my silent plea.

My son, did you know that your father is still alive?

"Yes, I want to see them."

"I'll give you two hours."

"Alone?"

"Yes, alone."

* * *

I must have really been in a bad state to have been granted such a favor. I saw them. They left us alone for two hours, together in a small waiting room. And for two hours I cried with Balthazar in my arms.

One-Way Ticket

Three weeks later I walked, light of step, into the white room that was Rome's Court of Appeals. It barely resembled the courts we have in France. It had modern decor (like the architecture of the building itself), its walls were engraved with abstract motifs and, most strikingly, everything—the judges' chambers, prisoners' docks, witness stands, lawyers' chairs, and public seats—was situated at the same level. There were no elevated platforms from which the judiciary powers crushed you, no perch from which the prosecutor looked down at you from above. An attention to equality and understanding was built into this space, if not our minds. It was still a circus, but less confined, more spacious, and less stiffened by the gravity of ritual.

I saw all of my loyal friends, celebrities and hippies, and I greeted them with a spring in my step to show them that I was in good spirits. Laura Betti came forward and touched my hand, as if to bring me luck. The judges also seemed brighter than those who had condemned me. They weren't green. Their skin was more beautiful, more luminous, and it seemed as though they were fueled by thought, more conscious of their responsibility, and that they were closer to the true work of judgement than to the punishing machine.

And they were probably impressed by the presence of television and radio reporters in the audience. It was extraordinary—the debates and the ruling would be broadcast throughout all of Italy. People were going to be able to see the workings of justice from up close. The ruling that would take place here, which would confirm or contradict the previous one, would have thousands of witnesses. The judges would be constantly confronted with their image, judged by it. They would no longer be amongst themselves, protected by their fortressed castles in which they were used to dealing with each other without anyone else knowing about their maneuvers. They were now going to have to judge with their true colors on display, naked for all to see.

The trial, the court, the ruling of justice—it's always a work of theatre. But there is a huge difference between a stage that is limited to relatives, to a small number of people in the audience, and one that is amplified and flashed upon thousands of screens. The judiciary sham takes on a different allure. The effects employed after ten years of practice don't come across the same way on screen. The actors must renew their repertoire of ticks and tricks. Stakes are raised when justice is served in public and people bear witness to it. The accused are no longer the ones in jeopardy. Instead the judges and the institution itself run the risk of appearing ridiculous and cruel.

The cameras were probably only there to provide suspense, drama, and even scandal to millions of viewers; they wouldn't have missed filming a soccer game or a war, either. But their presence had another effect: it radically transformed the nature and scope of representation, and that was a good thing—not only for the accused but for everyone, the judges and the audience—because it demystified the ceremony. "You saw the president's face?... Look, he just yawned...The prosecutor is a bad actor... They look so stupid with their robes..." I was pleased, because I imagined all the commentary abounding among Italian families, huddled together at dinnertime.

All shows can be somewhat alienating. But when it's life itself that is being filmed, through television reporting or what is known as cinéma-vérité, something rather miraculous can happen: masks fall, the hypocrisy of the powerful is revealed before everyone's eyes, and everyone can read the lying cowardice on the faces that pretend to be important. The trial, which begins as a show, is revealed to be a parody through the doubling that occurs in its filming. I was really counting on this, as well as on the possibility of having a platform from which I could go beyond the judges to address the people of this country.

"Let us begin. May the accused now respond to the Court's questions."

I summoned all the strength I had to speak a sufficiently intelligible Italian.

"If you want to begin, let's do it, and let's be sure we never stop. The truth is that justice ought to be more just. Prisoners are not re-educated in these prisons—they are systematically destroyed. Prisons are an industry of the State, and the coal that feeds this industry's heaters is made of the prisoners' very flesh."

"Let's stick to the facts of the trial. You are not here to hold a meeting, but to respond to our questions."

Of course it couldn't last. I'd nonetheless succeeded in saying some things that meant a lot to me and even the presiding judge, when he interrupted me, had been forced into a polite prudence that he wouldn't have displayed under normal circumstances. I sat down again. Until the verdict, the rest of the hearing wouldn't be that interesting—a mere repetition of the first trial.

I looked at my mother. She had sacrificed so much to be there; she had gotten a few days off from the hotel in Paris where she worked as a maid. There she was, timid and scared, her eyes focused on me.

The only link that remains sacred to me is the one that binds me to you, mother, who have struggled your entire life for our sake. We made you cry when we should have blessed you. I admire my mother for staying strong even when she was punished by the barbaric laws of an era that villainized young, unwed mothers. Despite the treacherous hypocrisy of a society that considered unmarried women to be dishonorable, you knew that life is more important than a morality that poisons people with its superstitions. You have now won against established order, even though my brother and I haven't stopped making you suffer. You paid for this victory with your time and your health, not to mention the insults that were aimed at you and the bad behavior of your sons, who were always at fault in one way or another. You're probably not surprised to see me here on this bench, even though it's the first trial you've ever seen. And in your simple faith you've probably prayed for this dark saga, which has followed me since adolescence, to finally come to an end.

Your wishes came true. Although you couldn't have understood the reading of the verdict, you must have known what it meant when the crowd applauded. "In the name of the people, under Articles 523 and 213 of the Penal Code of Procedure, the Roman Court of Appeals hereby annuls the preceding conviction, and finds Pierre André Clémenti to be not guilty of the charges that are held against him, due to insufficient evidence, and orders his immediate release. However, we call for the immediate arrest of Anna-Maria Lauricella."

My friends' cheers and cries of joy prevented me from fully hearing the final verdict, the most cruel and unjust end of all. How could I have been acquitted and Anna-Maria condemned? Living together, suspected together, arrested together, both of us imprisoned for the same reasons—but they send you back to your cell? I didn't understand anything, except that this discrepancy was an even crueler abuse than the imprisonment of two innocent people for a few more months. What was my absolution worth if it was at the price of your sorrow? I had expected everything except this Solomon's decision. I wanted us to receive the same verdict and be united, just as we had been in prison—I didn't want this horrible half-measure!

My friends surrounded me immediately, and soon I was issued

from the hands of riflemen and pushed forward into my mother's arms. But Anna-Maria, I caught your gaze before you looked away, and your eyes held me responsible for the inhuman cruelty of these judges!

But there came one more bad surprise. I hadn't taken three steps as a free man when two police officers asked me for one last formality. I had to accept the expulsion order initiated against me. I had twenty-four hours to leave Rome and they would even pay for my flight. I was undesirable and—this would never end!—"a danger to public order."

Even a verdict that is delivered in happiness, justice, and peace, can penalize, punish, and close what it had intended to open—as though the repressive machine is so powerful, so far gone, that even its so-called positive and liberating decisions cast a shadow, taste like misfortune, and injure those they pretend to save. Today I am struck by the fact that the system's logic is fundamentally negative, that even the dream of a more just justice is laughable because the system's repressiveness always supersedes its educational and liberating potential. Even on the rare occasion that liberating potential makes strides, these efforts are nonetheless restrained and diverted by the system. In this way, all innocents are potential criminals, all non-prisoners live in provisional freedom, and the acquitted are only ever freed on bail. Even when the system is forced to hand out a little freedom, it keeps what's essential for itself. The threat always looms, and it never lets up.

Dear Minister of Justice...

One day, I would like to tread once again on Italian soil and return to Rebibbia, to check in with the guys and see if they are still as rebellious, to make sure the warden hasn't forgotten those peaceful words from one of his children. I'd like to go back there, to act in a play in the great courtyard, or to project a film. Perhaps things will have changed, perhaps the prison bosses will have put some bricks aside, not for their seaside villas but to give a swimming pool to the prisoners so that they can, from time to time, swim a few laps in the water. It's so nice to swim, especially in Rome where the summer boils.

Perhaps the prisoners will be in charge at that point, and the prison will be a large, collectively managed community, and they will have organized daily classes about the problems that interest them, and even Rome's artists will come and teach at the Rebibbia School of Dramatic Arts. And Fellini will come to premier his films, and present Roma to two thousand prisoners—isn't that better than showing it to the Roman bourgeoisie? This way, these men can start to know why they are on this earth and in this prison, and they will learn that neither should be a place of condemnation and repression, but first and foremost a place of creation. They will have the chance to take life as it is—even and especially if it's in prison—and to seize this life in a creative and non-destructive way.

Don't say this is a utopian idea. This can actually happen. It will happen with the revolution. I met a lot of political activists in prison—in Italy, they are arrested under "common law." I talked with them a great deal. They know what prisons are, and they know who prisoners are, too. The political activists I've known don't partake in abstract political discourse, which goes over the heads of so many. They listened. They heard the complaints, the problems, and they gave their explanations of justice and repression. But more than anything they learned about prisoners and I think that they will know how to use what they learned. The Maoists (because it's largely Maoists in prison in Italy) say that to heal the malady you needn't kill the man.

But we don't have to wait for the revolutionary storm to break down prison's doors. We can act here and now. Obviously, so much is dependent on those whose careers allow them to get to know and see prison life from up close—priests, doctors, psychiatrists, lawyers, etc. Of course, they are more or less overseen by the penitentiary administration, who can make their jobs easy, or eliminate them, replace them, or blame them. But they nonetheless possess a substantial amount of power: the immense power of witness. You who have spent a part of your life among prisoners without actually being one—you have seen the intolerable. Unless you closed your eyes or plugged your ears, you saw. If you have the balls, speak up. If you think that the dignity of man is indivisible—that it isn't reserved for the powerful, for the rich, for those who are (still) free, and that the others, the poor, the exploited, the locked up, have the right to demand freedom—speak up. And you have the chance not only to speak, but to act, mobilize, and agitate those who don't know or who choose not to know. Do it. Don't wait anymore. What will it take for you to act? More revolts? They won't stop, and the prisoners who rise up are risking more than you. Suicides? There have already been more than thirty in French prisons since the start of the year. Is that not enough?

But I think about those who, comfortable in their little world, forget about the very existence of prisons. Of course, they are on the outside, and they don't do anything that would make them go to jail, or so they believe. I'm telling you, it's wrong to think of prison as simply the opposite of freedom, to understand imprisonment as the "taking away of freedom." This is the legal definition of the prison, but not the reality. To be locked up is not just to be deprived of one's freedom of movement, relationships, and distractions. In prison, you can move (if just a little), you can have relationships, and even distractions. It's not the limitations that are intolerable. Anyone who believes themselves to be free is in fact a prisoner of their own lifestyle and habits—their apartment, family, neighborhood, job, even their vacations. What's intolerable is that prison makes everyone a dead man. Each day it makes corpses, empty heads, and dead weights out of living flesh and active minds. Prison produces only the useless, the negative.

The great debate about the abolition of the death penalty is hypocritical, as if the choice were between death and life, not between an instant death versus an extended death, and a no less difficult one. Because prison is nothing but a slow killing machine—and by the way, it doesn't even take that long to kill you. If we were talking about prison abolition, things would be different. But to abolish the death penalty because it is "particularly barbarous and revolting" and trade it for life in prison—this merely gives you a good conscience for saving the head of someone who will suffer a more insidious torture. You saved a head, fine, but what's inside that head? What is it good for?

In case you didn't already know, let me tell you: in prison I learned that all men can be changed, and they change according to their conditions, depending on their environment, and all their thoughts, habits, and reflexes adapt according to the ground and climate in which they grow. Just as surely as prisons transform young delinquents into criminals, criminals into jailbirds, and jailbirds into dying men, prisons could transform their prisoners into useful citizens, and not into men who will hurt their brothers.

Anyone who doesn't care about prisons just because they are on the outside of them must know that their freedom has been bought at the price of others' oppression and suffering—and this freedom is costly. They ought to know that they live on the tip of a volcano whose slumber grows more restless by the day. And one day, when prisons explode, the old ways of society will go up in flames, too. The boiler can no longer bear this growing pressure inside it.

You can, from the inside and from the outside, influence prison management, as well as the administering of justice and penalties. What some make, others work to unmake. What some hide, others can expose. Don't give free rein to modern executioners. The prison camps in South Vietnam or the fortresses in Brazil aren't the only places where there's torture going on. We should clean up our own house.

Let's talk about the guards, for instance. In France and Italy, the unions say, "We are workers like anyone else, we have our problems and our demands." Sure, because these are workers like any other, let's talk to them. Why should prisoners be the only ones to talk to the guards? We should talk to them a little about what they are here for, because even if they are trained to beat up any prisoner, it doesn't mean they have any interest in doing so. They are the victims of the same system they work for. But now I'm just dreaming.

Dear Minister of Justice, I dream about you. One evening when you're in your bed, I would like to find you awake in the grips of insomnia, with nothing to do, and no way to slip back into sleep. You've got problems and you are suffering: all this power at your disposal, and no clue how to use it! They called you from all around the country—nothing is working out in the prisons, nor in the courts, and no one is happy. The prisoners are complaining, as are the guards. The judges and the judged. And all of that comes back to you. You thrash in bed and you don't know what to do, finding neither sleep nor the solution. Too busy? Overworked? Not only that. You also lack imagination, and at the heart of it all you find no pleasure in the work that has been entrusted to you. There are riots everywhere, protests, and a meal skipped for a hunger strike at the very moment you try, in vain, to fall asleep. And the only idea you have is to lock them all up! Those who are outside, go inside. Those who are inside, go to solitary. You think that if you lock up your nightmares, you'll feel better.

You think you represent justice in this country. But are you up to it? Serving justice is a sacred thing. You can heal or destroy. You have the choice; you are the minister. Perhaps it's this power that troubles your sleep. You can throw more and more men into despair. The weak are defenseless in your hands. You could choose to illuminate their minds. But you don't do it, and this eats away at you. Do you remember last Christmas? There was a darkness that hung over the day, perhaps even shadowing the eyes of your children. You had withheld gifts from your immense family of prisoners. Why do you always have such bad ideas?

* * *

One sleepless night around midnight, I think it would be good for you to take your car and drive to La Santé Prison and see what happens there. I'm sure they would open the doors for you. Sometimes all you have to do is state your name at the door. Come in, turn on the lights, and see your nighttime hauntings from up close. Take in this world where everything could change and be reinvented. Do not despair. Breathe and create. I salute you.

AFTERWORD

There is loss—and then there is the loss of Pierre. He was beautiful and mysterious, half-angel and half-demon, so dark and so bright at the same time.
He was a visionary, a non-conformist without concession.
You were Pure. Pure until death, and an angel forever.
To an entire generation, you exemplify a fugitive passage that few artists have made: a life wholly dedicated to Art and Creation.
You said no to Maestro Fellini, as no other actor ever dared.
You refused the most tempting offers, either from famous directors or for enormous sums of money; instead you preferred to eclipse your star status, opt for creativity, and support the work of young directors.
These movies, once considered minor, have become (thanks to you) cult classics.
You were an artist imprisoned for your lack of conformity; like Caravaggio in his cell, you painted the heavenly light that opened up the spiritual song of poetry. And you gave us this brightness through your work.
You expressed your critical thoughts—your freedom was found in their expression. You remain an example for future generations of how to realize oneself in life and in art.
You left us on December 27, 1999, during a period of raging storms, to join the angels above.
We miss you.

—Balthazar Clémenti
May 2005

A Note About the Author

PIERRE CLÉMENTI was born in 1942 in Paris. He was an actor, director, and icon of French counterculture. Perhaps best known for his role opposite Catherine Deneuve in Louis Buñuel's *Belle de Jour* (1967), Clémenti was also a muse for many Italian directors, acting in *The Leopard* (Visconti, 1963), *Pigsty* (Pasolini, 1969), *The Cannibals* (Cavani, 1970), *Partner* and *The Conformist* (Bertolucci, 1968 and 1970). In 1971, he was arrested for drug possession while living in Rome, and was imprisoned for eighteen months while awaiting trial. Clémenti and many others were convinced that he was unjustly targeted because of his politics and fierce rejection of mainstream culture, and the charges were eventually dropped due to insufficient evidence. Over the course of his life, Clémenti also directed several experimental films, such as *Visa de Censure Numéro X* (1975), *The Revolution is Only a Beginning: Let's Continue Fighting* (1968), *New Old* (1979), and *The Sun* (1988). Clémenti died in 1999 at the age of fifty-seven.

A Note About the Translator

CLAIRE FOSTER is a literary translator and bookseller living in Toronto. *A Few Personal Messages* is her first full-length translation.

The translator would like to thank Gabriel Briex for his invaluable contributions to the translation.